Dear Reader,

Does a marriage of convenience appeal to you?
Any woman who thinks it's just a practical
arrangement is going to get more than she
bargained for. To me, marriage comes with
certain expectations. Many of them on the
wedding night.

Since my business required I leave my
bachelorhood behind, marrying the boss's
daughter seemed the ideal way to gain a wife.
Too bad she had a prenuptial contract that
didn't include a clause for the role she'd been
playing in my dreams.

By the time Heather Strand and I make it to the
altar, the Arizona desert heat will seem like a
cool breeze.

Jake Cavender

Arizona

1. ALABAMA
Full House • Jackie Weger
2. ALASKA
Borrowed Dreams • Debbie Macomber
3. ARIZONA
Call It Destiny • Jayne Ann Krentz
4. ARKANSAS
Another Kind of Love • Mary Lynn Baxter
5. CALIFORNIA
Deceptions • Annette Broadrick
6. COLORADO
Stormwalker • Dallas Schulze
7. CONNECTICUT
Straight from the Heart • Barbara Delinsky
8. DELAWARE
Author's Choice • Elizabeth August
9. FLORIDA
Dream Come True • Ann Major
10. GEORGIA
Way of the Willow • Linda Shaw
11. HAWAII
Tangled Lies • Anne Stuart
12. IDAHO
Rogue's Valley • Kathleen Creighton
13. ILLINOIS
Love by Proxy • Diana Palmer
14. INDIANA
Possibles • Lass Small
15. IOWA
Kiss Yesterday Goodbye • Leigh Michaels
16. KANSAS
A Time To Keep • Curtiss Ann Matlock
17. KENTUCKY
One Pale, Fawn Glove • Linda Shaw
18. LOUISIANA
Bayou Midnight • Emilie Richards
19. MAINE
Rocky Road • Anne Stuart
20. MARYLAND
The Love Thing • Dixie Browning
21. MASSACHUSETTS
Pros and Cons • Bethany Campbell
22. MICHIGAN
To Tame a Wolf • Anne McAllister
23. MINNESOTA
Winter Lady • Janet Joyce
24. MISSISSIPPI
After the Storm • Rebecca Flanders
25. MISSOURI
Choices • Annette Broadrick

26. MONTANA
Part of the Bargain • Linda Lael Miller
27. NEBRASKA
Secrets of Tyrone • Regan Forest
28. NEVADA
Nobody's Baby • Barbara Bretton
29. NEW HAMPSHIRE
Natural Attraction • Marisa Carroll
30. NEW JERSEY
Moments Harsh, Moments Gentle • Joan Hohl
31. NEW MEXICO
Within Reach • Marilyn Pappano
32. NEW YORK
In Good Faith • Judith McWilliams
33. NORTH CAROLINA
The Security Man • Dixie Browning
34. NORTH DAKOTA
A Class Act • Kathleen Eagle
35. OHIO
Too Near the Fire • Lindsay McKenna
36. OKLAHOMA
A Time and a Season • Curtiss Ann Matlock
37. OREGON
Uneasy Alliance • Jayne Ann Krentz
38. PENNSYLVANIA
The Wrong Man • Ann Major
39. RHODE ISLAND
The Bargain • Patricia Coughlin
40. SOUTH CAROLINA
The Last Frontier • Rebecca Flanders
41. SOUTH DAKOTA
For Old Times' Sake • Kathleen Eagle
42. TENNESSEE
To Love a Dreamer • Ruth Langan
43. TEXAS
For the Love of Mike • Candace Schuler
44. UTAH
To Tame the Hunter • Stephanie James
45. VERMONT
Finders Keepers • Carla Neggers
46. VIRGINIA
The Devlin Dare • Cathy Gillen Thacker
47. WASHINGTON
The Waiting Game • Jayne Ann Krentz
48. WEST VIRGINIA
All in the Family • Heather Graham Pozzessere
49. WISCONSIN
Starstruck • Anne McAllister
50. WYOMING
Special Touches • Sharon Brondos

MEN MADE IN AMERICA

JAYNE ANN KRENTZ

Call It Destiny

Arizona

Harlequin Books

TORONTO • NEW YORK • LONDON
AMSTERDAM • PARIS • SYDNEY • HAMBURG
STOCKHOLM • ATHENS • TOKYO • MILAN
MADRID • WARSAW • BUDAPEST • AUCKLAND

HARLEQUIN ENTERPRISES LTD.
225 Duncan Mill Road, Don Mills,
Ontario, Canada M3B 3K9

1

IT WOULD BE AN HONEST sort of marriage; a marriage based on shared goals and shared business interests; a marriage with the potential for friendship between the two parties involved; a comfortable marriage that would please the relatives.

It was going to be a marriage of convenience.

"I've brought along a draft of the prenuptial agreement. Take your time looking it over and after you've signed it, I'll hand it over to the attorney. She'll make certain we both have valid copies." Heather Strand sipped her perfectly chilled Napa Valley Chardonnay and smiled pleasantly across the gleaming white linen tablecloth at the man sitting opposite her. A hovering waiter, sensing that his presence was not needed at the moment, discreetly disappeared in the direction of the kitchen.

A part of Heather's lively brain absently noted and approved the waiter's discretion. She appreciated well-trained staff. "If you have any questions, I'll be happy to go over the details with you," Heather continued when her dinner partner said nothing. Jake Cavender seemed momentarily more interested in his scallop soufflé than in the business of their marriage.

"I'm certain you'll have everything in order," he murmured. "You seem to be a very well-organized woman."

Heather inclined her sleek head with its bronzed brown hair that curved with elegant neatness behind her ears. The heavy mass was well styled, cut with blunt precision to fall just even with the line of her jaw.

"I try," she responded dryly, not quite certain how to take Cavender's comments. She didn't know him all that well yet, and there were occasions when she couldn't be certain that he wasn't subtly mocking her.

"I understand from your father that you didn't always."

"Try to be organized?" Heather shrugged faintly. The movement caused the fabric of her narrow, raspberry-colored chemise to shift silkily. "No, I suppose I didn't. It annoyed my father when I approached everything in an off-the-wall style," she confided cheerfully.

"And annoying your father was a prime consideration?" Jake poured himself a little more of the Chardonnay, his cool gray eyes examining her composed face.

"As I'm sure you know by now, my father and I did not get along well when I was in my teens. My mother's theory is that my father and I were a little too much alike temperamentally. I'm afraid it was a classic case of youthful rebellion."

"Bordering on outright warfare, according to your younger sisters."

Heather's eyes narrowed. This man's easy familiarity with her family was disconcerting at times. There were moments when she thought he knew her relatives better than she did. But then she'd been living in California for the past several years with only occasional trips back to Tucson.

"Don't be concerned with my colorful past," Heather advised politely. "I assure you I've outgrown it."

"Have you?"

Heather shot him a chilled glance. "Believe me, in my wild impetuous youth I would not have dreamed of getting involved in a business marriage!"

Cavender smiled at her. Heather was getting accustomed to that smile with its faint twist of amused speculation. She didn't quite understand it yet, but she was getting used to it. "Why have you come back to Tucson, Heather?"

"You know the answer to that." Heather smiled briefly at the waiter as he appeared to remove the soufflé dishes. When the young man disappeared she met Jake Cavender's eyes. "My father is retiring and I'm prepared to step into his shoes."

"You had an excellent career in the hotel business already carved out for yourself in San Francisco. What can your father's hotel here in Tucson offer that can compete with what you had established in California?"

"A chance to be in total control; make my own decisions without having to get them approved; implement some of my own ideas. San Francisco and San Diego were excellent training grounds, Jake. I learned a great deal. I'm ready now to assume the responsibilities of running Hacienda Strand."

"You could have returned to Tucson a few years ago and learned everything you needed to know by working at your father's side."

"My father and I could never have worked side by side, especially not when I was younger." Heather's mouth curved ruefully. "It was unfortunate for him that I was the only one in the family who really had an interest in the hotel business. Neither of my sisters wanted any part of running the Hacienda, so Dad was stuck trying to groom me. But we seemed to clash on almost everything. Even now I doubt a partnership would work. He knows that or else he wouldn't have made it clear that he intends to stay out of the business entirely now."

Heather looked approvingly down at the delicate veal-and-mushroom dish being placed in front of her. Cavender had ordered the lamb, and from the deferential manner in which the entrée was placed in front of him, she knew the waiter recognized him. Heather understood perfectly, of course. For the past two years Jake Cavender had been Paul Strand's right-hand man. Cavender was, according to Heather's father, a genius with numbers. The Hacienda Strand had never been in better shape financially, and Paul was quick to credit Cavender for the sound financial strength of the resort.

And since everyone in the hotel-and-restaurant business in Tucson knew and respected Paul Strand, it followed that Strand's right-hand man was also recognized when he chose to dine out. It wasn't at all odd, Heather reflected in silent amusement, that no one recognized her. She had changed since she had left Tucson.

"You must know that your parents are delighted you've decided to return," Jake remarked casually. "They're proud of what you've accomplished in California, naturally, but they've been hoping for a long time that you'd make the decision to come back to the Hacienda."

"I could never have returned unless I had managed to achieve something for myself in California." Heather smiled, her hazel eyes deliberately bland and unreadable. "I left Tucson under something resembling a cloud."

"I've heard the story," Jake remarked sardonically. "You were last seen heading west on the back of a black Yamaha motorcycle. I believe your sister Liz said you had vowed to marry the guy who was driving the bike before you reached California."

Heather felt a distasteful chill. Jake Cavender, it seemed, had indeed been adopted into the family circle. "Rick and I planned to detour through Nevada for a quick ceremony before we headed on to California," she explained crisply. Not that it was any of Jake's business. It was just that he appeared to know so much already it didn't seem to matter if he knew some of the rest.

"Rick?"

"That was the name of the guy driving the Yamaha." Heather regarded her companion. "Didn't Liz tell you that little detail? His full name was Rick Monroe and he was every adolescent's fantasy of a cool, handsome, reckless boyfriend. I was eighteen at the time and he was twenty-four. And he looked terrific in biker leather," Heather concluded with a quick grin.

"A real leader of the pack, hmm?" Cavender didn't appear either amused or indulgent. Instead there was a faint shadow of disgust in his gray gaze.

That shadow was enough to ignite some of the old spirit of rebellion in Heather, much to her surprise. She had assumed that element of her nature was well and truly buried in her past. Why did this man have the power to stir the ashes? Her berry-tinted nails drummed restlessly on the white tablecloth. When Jake's eyes dropped to her hand she ceased the action abruptly and quickly regained her aloof poise.

"No, Rick was not a 'leader of the pack.' He was a loner. Much like me, I thought at the time."

"You were hardly a loner," Jake said. "You had the full protection and support of a loving family. Two sisters, your mother and father and several aunts and uncles and cousins. No, you didn't qualify as a loner at eighteen, Heather."

Heather blinked uneasily, her long lashes sweeping down to hide the annoyed reaction that surely would be reflected in her eyes. Jake Cavender could be a trifle blunt at times. Magnanimously she assumed it was one of the reasons he had been so useful to her father and would continue to be useful to her. A good executive did not want to surround herself with yes-men. On the other hand, there was such a thing as tact, especially in a man who has just agreed to marriage.

"Whatever happened when I was eighteen really doesn't concern you, does it?" She put him in his place with a quelling little smile and delicately took a bite of the minted artichoke hearts that accompanied her veal.

"I beg your pardon," he said quietly. "Did I stray over the line?"

"Yes. Do you make a habit of doing it?"

Jake considered the question and then nodded his head once. "I'm afraid so. I'm not particularly good at handling people."

"You're in a strange line of work for someone who isn't good at dealing with people."

"Hotel work? It is a little off base, isn't it? But it's worked out very well for me. Your father always took the role of jovial host with the guests and mediated with the members of the staff when it was necessary. I dealt with the business side of things. The financial facts and figures."

"It seems to have been a highly workable arrangement," Heather said bracingly. "I assume the same arrangement will work between us."

"I'm sure it will," Jake retorted smoothly.

"You have no objections to the prenuptial agreement?" Heather experienced a sudden need to pin him down. There was an elusive quality to this relationship and, being fashioned of talented executive material, she wanted to define and control it. Instinct.

"I think it's unnecessary, but if you feel more comfortable having such a contract between us, then I'm perfectly willing to sign. Did you have a contract with your young punk?"

Heather's eyes chilled. "As it happens, Rick and I were never married. And if you don't mind, Jake, I prefer not to discuss that situation. It's in the past. If the actions of my youth offend you, I suggest you reconsider my offer of marriage."

"Your family would be crushed if I did that," he said with one of his quick unreadable smiles.

"Yes," she agreed. "My family would be devastated. You've certainly made an impression on my parents and both my sisters, as well as all the other assorted relatives. In two years you've practically become a member of the family, haven't you?"

"Practically, but not quite." Jake helped himself to a slice of French bread, spreading it liberally with butter. His concentration was devoted to the small task and, as Heather was learning, when he gave his attention to something he tended to focus completely on the matter until it was finished.

"Is that why you're marrying me, Jake?" Heather demanded in a spurt of perception. "To become a full member of the family?"

He set down the buttered bread and lifted his intent gaze to meet hers. "I think it's part of the reason, yes. Does that worry you?"

It was Heather's turn to consider a question. "I don't see why it should. I know very well that I was never the son and heir my father longed to groom to take his place. It's quite natural that he's begun to see you as a substitute during the past couple of years. You're devoted to Hacienda Strand and you're very good at what you do. When you failed to panic at the idea of marrying me, he probably thought he was finally living in the best of all possible worlds. His wayward daughter had returned to assume her preordained role as president of Hacienda Strand, Inc., and his handpicked son was willing to become her consort and faithful assistant. A nice neat package."

"You don't seem to have any objections to being part of that nice neat package," Jake observed mildly.

"I'm no longer eighteen and determined to rebel against all authority."

"You're twenty-nine and willing to submit to authority?" Jake taunted lightly.

Heather laughed. "Hardly. I'm twenty-nine and in charge of my own life. I know what I want and I have firmly established in everyone's mind that I'm capable of getting what I want on my own without my father's help. I'm back in Tucson to take over my father's hotel, Jake, but I'm back on my own terms."

"From what I've heard you left on your own terms, too."

"The world looks different at twenty-nine than it did at eighteen," Heather told him firmly.

"And it will no doubt look different again at thirty-eight."

"Is that how old you are?"

"Yes. Why? Don't I look my age?" he asked dryly.

Heather surveyed the liberal slivers of gray in the thick teak darkness of his conservatively trimmed hair. Jake Cavender looked his age, all right. In fact, he could probably have passed for forty. There was a hardness in him that implied experience; the kind of experience that made a man look as if he'd never been a child. For the first time Heather began to wonder about his past.

"Fortunately for men, looking their age at thirty-eight is not a handicap," she temporized lightly.

"Then you're not exactly marrying me for my looks, are you?" he asked with a wry slanting smile.

No, Heather thought, she wasn't marrying him for his looks. After her experience with Rick Monroe she was unlikely to make the mistake of being attracted to any man on the basis of physical appearance. But even if she hadn't learned the hard way that you couldn't judge a man on that level, would she, in all honesty, have been attracted to Jake Cavender? He wasn't a handsome man.

It was not, however, his bluntly carved face that caught one's attention. It was the cool assessing intelligence in those gray eyes that demanded first notice. Later a woman saw the heavy pelt of teak-shaded hair, noted the solid lean body and wondered about the grim brackets around his mouth. But it was the gray gaze that made one stop and think. He was not the kind of man a woman wanted for an enemy. His anger would not be loud and flamboyant. It would be cold and merciless. Just as well, Heather decided, that she was going to be the ranking partner in this marriage of convenience. Her status as the one in charge of the luxurious resort hotel her father had founded would insulate her from whatever masculine temperament and ego Jake Cavender indulged.

It was one thing to yell at one's wife; quite another to yell at one's boss!

"I don't think either of us is entering this marriage with any ridiculous romantic illusions," Heather said softly. "I know I certainly have no interest in a marriage based on the traditional fantasies. I've learned to be a realist in the past few years. I think you probably are one, too. I see no reason why we shouldn't get along very well together."

"You expect us to function as a team?" Jake concentrated on the beautifully prepared lamb.

"I expect us to function very much as the kind of team you and my father made." *With me, of course, being the one in charge,* Heather added silently. That part was very important. No need to stress it aloud to Jake, however. He knew his position in the hierarchy. Presumably he knew his position in the marriage, too. But just in case he didn't, she'd spelled it all out in black and white in the prenuptial agreement she had handed to him earlier.

"Your father and I weren't exactly married to each other."

"Our being married shouldn't make any difference in how the hotel is run."

Jake watched her for a few seconds. She could almost feel the way he was adding up the information he had about her and was putting it through the computer he called a brain. "You're right," he finally said. "Our being married won't make the slightest bit of difference in how the Hacienda Strand is run. More wine?"

Heather brushed aside an odd sensation of unease and smiled her most charming smile. "Thank you." She held out her glass, her eyes softening above the rim as she relaxed again. "I have great hopes for this marriage, actually," she confided lightly. "It's based on all the right things. We have the unifying interest of the hotel, for example. In the past few years I've come to realize just how sound an idea it is for husbands and wives to be able to share their work interests. Such ties seem much more durable than bonds based on romantic fluff, don't you think? I've witnessed several divorces in which the man left his wife to marry his secretary simply because the work he had shared with the 'other woman' had built a stronger relationship than the marriage he had shared with his wife."

Jake gave her an odd glance. "In other words, you feel we have a basis for companionship?"

"Exactly." Heather took another sip of wine and reflected on the subject she herself had brought up. "This marriage will also be very comfortable in a lot of other ways. My parents love you."

"That's important to you?"

"It wasn't when I was eighteen but now, yes, it's more important. It will just make things so much easier."

"When your father told me he had suggested the idea of us getting married, I half expected to hear you'd gone through the roof. Based on what I'd been told of your character I assumed a more or less arranged marriage would bring out all the old spirit of rebellion. I told Paul he'd made one hell of a mistake. That's when he informed me that you were a changed woman."

"You sound as if you don't believe in the change," she returned, mildly irritated by his skepticism. She'd seen traces of it frequently during the two weeks she'd been back in Tucson on a permanent basis, but tonight it seemed more pronounced. "I assure you I'm not the wild child who left here all those years ago. What's the matter, Jake?" she added, unable to resist the small taunt. "Worried that you'll find yourself married to a first-class shrew?"

"I'm sure my only problem at the moment is that I've got a case of wedding jitters," Jake said, refusing to rise to the bait. But he wasn't looking at her as he spoke. He was focusing intently on the last of his bread.

For some reason the fact that he wasn't meeting her eyes bothered Heather. She didn't know Jake well, but she had been around him often enough in the past couple of weeks, spent enough time with him during the past eighteen months or so on her occasional visits home, to learn his mannerisms. He was usually very direct.

"Somehow you don't seem the type to get jitters," she murmured. "But I think you might have a few genuine reservations about marrying me. That's only logical. You're a financial wizard, however, so why not look at this whole proposition the way you'd look at a Hacienda Strand spread sheet? On the plus side you will be marrying the boss. That's always been considered a bright thing to do. You'll be cementing your position in my family and in the family business. You have my word the marriage will not be a volatile affair. I'm really quite a placid individual these days. I'm a hard worker, diplomatic with guests and staff, and I honor my word. I can guarantee there will be no embarrassing public brawls or arguments. There won't be any private ones, either, for that matter. I'm healthy, reasonably intelligent, tidy and punctual. I don't lose my temper anymore the way I did when I was younger, and I'm always willing to listen to all sides of an issue before I make up my mind. I've been told I'm a very good boss," she concluded with a quick grin.

Jake stared at her for a long moment and Heather wished suddenly that she could read his thoughts. That polite mask he wore gave little clue to what he was really feeling.

"And on the negative side?" he finally asked softly.

Heather narrowed her eyes. "There are no negatives. At least no major ones come to mind."

"Amazing. That certainly makes things simple, doesn't it?" But he was smiling again; that wry curve to his hard mouth that he'd favored her with so frequently during the past couple of weeks. She wished it didn't give her a pang of uncertainty every time she saw it.

"Very simple," she assured him briskly.

"And have you also worked out a balance sheet for yourself?"

"Of course."

"I'd like to hear the items in the plus column, if you don't mind."

"Why not?" she said airily. "This marriage will provide me with a husband eminently suitable to my whole family. I will be marrying a man who knows and understands my work and who will share it with me. I am assured by all who know him that I will be getting a husband who has no reputation for violence." Heather looked at her escort with amusement. "Mother says you aren't likely to be a wife beater."

"How reassuring for both of us."

"Isn't it? Let's see, what else will I be getting out of this marriage? Oh, yes, I mustn't overlook the fact that both parties are going into it with a full understanding of the situation. We needn't bother with a lot of romantic fiction nor do we have to convince ourselves that we are passionately in love. Our relationship will be allowed to grow naturally, without any undue pressure."

"Our relationship sounds like some sort of experimental germ growing in a culture dish." But Jake didn't appear at all perturbed.

Impulsively Heather leaned forward, her fingertips coming to rest lightly on the sleeve of his summerweight jacket. "I really do have great hopes for this arrangement, Jake. I think everything is going to be perfect."

His gray eyes went from her tinted nails to the earnest expression on her face. "I'm not sure about perfect," he hedged gently, "but it's bound to be interesting. Would you care for dessert?"

Withdrawing her hand, Heather shook her head. "No, thank you."

"Then perhaps we should be going. It's been a long day for you and I imagine you're tired." Jake signaled for the check, which was delivered almost immediately. He handled the details of paying the bill with casual efficiency, and then politely got to his feet and held Heather's chair.

She was vividly aware of his presence behind her as they made their way out of the restaurant and into the balmy summer evening. It was nearly the end of August and one of the typical summer thunderstorms had been and gone during the hour and a half Heather and Jake had been in the restaurant. As usual, a great deal of water had been dropped from the skies in a short period of time and the parking lot and the cars glittered

with it in the fresh aftermath of the rain. Jake's white
Mercedes had endured the sudden drenching with polite stoicism and Heather slid comfortably into the red
leather interior. A small river of water still coursed
down the specially designed channel between the
parking lot and the street, but the car splashed through
it easily. Soon all traces of the heavy storm would dis-
appear and Tucson would once again bake in the heat
of August.

"The rains have seemed heavier than usual this year,"
Heather remarked, more for something to say than any
other reason. Jake had been very silent since taking the
wheel.

"Perhaps they just seem heavier to you because
you've been away from Tucson so long," he suggested.

"Perhaps." Heather lapsed back into silence.

This time it was Jake who broke the quiet. "Is it good
to be home, Heather?"

"Yes," she affirmed with satisfaction. "Very good."

"Do you regret leaving?"

With a sigh, she shook her head. "At the time there
didn't seem to be much choice. Our home had become
a battleground. My father and I fought constantly and
my mother and sisters were forced to endure the warfare from the sidelines. It was very unpleasant. If I'd
stayed and gone to school here at the university there
would have been more of the same problems. Dad was
determined to direct my life and I was just as determined to do things my way. I insisted on challenging
him on every score, I'm afraid. His fury over my relationship with Rick Monroe was the last straw for both
of us."

"You took a course in hotel administration in California?"

"Oh, yes. Running a hotel is in my blood, I'm afraid. There was never any question in my mind that I would make a career in the hotel business. But I also knew I could never be part of Hacienda Strand as long as my father was in charge. We would have clashed on every issue."

"Who financed your education in California? The infamous Rick Monroe?" Jake asked the question with seeming lightness but Heather sensed a certain grimness buried in the words. Again she felt more than a trace of annoyance.

Quashing the faint stirrings of her long-dormant temper, Heather tried to answer the question patiently, as if it didn't really matter. "I financed my own education. Rick didn't have a dime to his name, I'm afraid. Lots of rebel-without-a-cause charm and some interesting ambitions, but no money. We parted ways before we even reached California."

Jake's head came around sharply in surprise. "You did?"

"I didn't have much choice. Not after I realized Rick's primary interest in me was my father's money. Actually, I think I knew it all along subconsciously and didn't want to admit it. He and the bike made for a dramatic exit from Tucson, but when he started demanding that I phone home for money I told him to get lost."

"And did he?"

"Yes. Unfortunately he took the bike. I had to hitch-hike to California." Heather forced a superficial laugh to cover the memories of fear and loneliness that had assaulted her on the traumatic trip. No one, she was convinced, understood isolation and loneliness until they'd stood alone on a dusty highway with only a few dollars in their pocket and a fierce determination not to run home for protection.

She'd been lucky. The truck driver who'd given her a lift had turned out to be a true gentleman of the road instead of a lecher. Thirty years her senior, he'd assumed a protective attitude toward her at the truck stops, let her doze in the sleeper compartment while he drove and insisted she was going to ruin her ears with pop music. He'd given her a crash course in the history of country-and-western music as an antidote, playing the country channels endlessly on the radio. Heather still retained a secret affection for the earthy stuff, which had not worn off in the intervening years.

"Being on the road isn't particularly romantic, is it?" Jake guided the Mercedes toward the foothills outside Tucson where the Hacienda Strand was located.

"No."

"But your pride wouldn't let you come home?"

"I couldn't come home. Not until I'd shown everyone I could take care of myself and that I didn't need Dad's money to cushion the way," she explained starkly.

"So how did you finance your hotel course?"

"Got a job in a fast-food hamburger place. No benefits and low salary but the road to the manager's job was wide open for anyone who wanted to work the bad hours. I became manager in three months," Heather said calmly. "After that, money was less of a problem. I didn't get a lot of sleep for the next couple of years but

I got one heck of an education. I can manufacture forty hamburgers a minute or supervise a gourmet hotel kitchen."

"You did things the hard way," Jake growled. "All because you were too headstrong to appreciate what your family wanted to give you."

Something snapped briefly inside Heather. She had been doing him the courtesy of answering some very personal questions and in return she sensed she was getting barely concealed disparagement and condemnation. She intended to put a stop to it in a hurry. Her hazel eyes flared in the dimly lit interior of the car.

"Let's get something straight, Jake. My past is absolutely no concern of yours, just as your past doesn't particularly interest me. I am not the wild and reckless girl I was when I left town. I am a mature adult woman who has achieved a considerable degree of success on her own. The decision to come back to Tucson is based on a number of factors but none of those factors includes financial need or career development. I had everything I needed or wanted in regard to those two items back in California. One last time, Jake, I'm here on my own terms and everything I do in my life is on my own terms. If you can't handle my past then say so now."

His fingers might have tightened briefly on the steering wheel; in the darkness Heather couldn't be certain. But Jake only hesitated a few seconds before saying quietly, "I can handle your past. It's not a whole hell of a lot different than my own."

Heather, her mouth open for further pithy comments, blinked and then said, "Really?"

"Except that there was no female version of Rick Monroe to sweep me away in grand style and there was no loving financially secure family to back me up if I ever got into more trouble than I could handle." The words were flat, not inviting further discussion.

Heather considered the man beside her, aware of the harshly carved profile and the controlled strength in the lean tough body. She decided not to ask the flood of questions that popped into her mind. Both of them were entitled to some privacy. After all, they still knew so little about each other.

The subdued roar of a black-and-chrome motorcycle followed the Mercedes into the elegant curving driveway of the Hacienda Strand. As Jake parked the car in one of the managers' slots, Heather turned to glance over her shoulder, smiling in quick pleasure. Before Jake could open his door she was already out on the white graveled path, waving at the young man who was parking the bike nearby.

"Hey, Jim," she called, hurrying forward. "It's beautiful! When did you get it?"

Jim Connors, a busboy in the hotel restaurant, grinned proudly as he carefully balanced the heavy motorcycle and withdrew the keys. "I took delivery this morning. What do you think? Ever seen anything like it before in your life?"

Jake had moved silently up behind Heather who was eyeing the bike with vast appreciation. "Quite a bike, Jim," he remarked soberly.

"Thank you, Mr. Cavender. I figure it's only going to take me the rest of my life to pay it off, but it's worth it!" Jim stowed the helmet he had worn behind the seat.

"I'm glad to see you had the sense to buy a helmet too," Jake observed approvingly.

"Yeah. My dad said it was the only way he'd agree to cosign the loan I had to get. I guess he's right, but it does take some of the excitement out of riding."

"I know what you mean," Heather murmured wistfully as she gently stroked the gleaming black fender of the big bike. "There's nothing like the feel of the wind in your hair."

"How about the bugs in your teeth?" Jake interrupted, his eyes narrowing as he watched Heather touch the motorcycle.

Jim chuckled. "You've got a point there. Oh, well. Buying the bike did give me an excuse to buy a black leather jacket. Mom wouldn't let me have one until she found out that it's another form of protection, like the helmet."

"It looks terrific," Heather said admiringly as Jim unfastened the heavy jacket. "A bit warm on a night like this, though."

"You take it easy on those streets, Jim," Jake began with a frown. "Motorcycles and wet pavement don't mix well."

Jim's enthusiasm was quickly masked as he heard the lecturing tone in Jake's voice. "Yes, sir, Mr. Cavender. I'm being real careful with the bike. The last thing I want to do is wreck it before it's even paid for. Well, excuse me, I'm a little late." The young man flashed a fleeting grin at Heather. "I'll be glad to give you a ride sometime, Miss Strand."

"Thank you, Jim. I'd love it," Heather assured him warmly. As the busboy hurried off, she rounded on

Jake. "There was no need to lecture him. I'm sure his parents have already given him any number of sermons on the subject of driving motorcycles."

"Well, he's certainly not going to get any words of wisdom from you, is he?" Jake noted evenly as he walked her toward her private cottage. Set some distance from the hotel itself, the charming structure, done in an adobe style with a wide front porch, afforded privacy and convenience. Jake used a similar cottage located across the garden. Heather's parents had an elegant home with a lovely private terrace that overlooked the beautifully kept grounds of the resort. "You looked ready to grab the keys and go joyriding."

"It's been a long time," Heather explained gently, secretly amused at his stern tone. "The black Yamaha I told you about? The one on which I made my escape from Tucson and Rick took when we parted ways?"

"What about it?"

"It was mine. Bought with the money I'd earned working in the hotel restaurant during my senior year in high school. I know exactly what kind of battle Jim had to wage to get his parents' permission to buy the bike. Just imagine what I had to go through! My mother nearly fainted and my father yelled for a week before giving in. I loved that bike. On it I felt wild and free and totally independent." Heather lifted her head in remembered pleasure, inhaling the rain-freshened air and closing her eyes briefly in recollection. "It was a fantastic feeling."

"And then you went to California and found out what it really feels like to be free and totally independent, hmm?" There was an acidly repressive tone to

Jake's words as he politely took the keys from her hand and opened her door.

"Ah, Jake. You do have a way of bringing things down to a more mundane level, don't you?" No wonder the man didn't consider himself adept at dealing with people. He wasn't! "Don't worry. As I've been assuring you all evening, I'm a changed woman." She reached out to pluck her keys from his hand. "You'll see just how realistic and businesslike I am these days when you read that prenuptial agreement."

"I'll go over it tonight," he promised, not moving from her threshold as she stepped inside. The intent considering gleam was back in his gray eyes as he stood. watching her a moment longer in silence.

With a spark of purely feminine intuition, Heather knew he was about to kiss her. The thought took her by surprise but she found the notion not at all unpleasant. In fact there was a definite sense of anticipation beginning to simmer in her bloodstream. A curious longing to gain some hint of what a real marriage to this man would be like. She had come to realize one could not cover so many details in a prenuptial agreement.

Jake stepped forward abruptly, tilting her chin with strong fingers. The gray gaze reflected a hint of silver fire that caught Heather off guard. Passion was not something she had expected to find in Jake Cavender. Perhaps she had been wrong. She felt the power in his hand and an unfamiliar wave of excitement washed through her. Love and desire were not items she had expected to find in her arrangement with Jake. The prospect of such a potential was both dizzying and a little frightening.

Heather's lashes settled lightly against her cheek as she allowed him to lift her face for his kiss. She sensed his nearness, felt the heat of his body only inches from hers. The sensation of his mouth hovering above her lips made the breath catch for an instant in her throat. An inexplicable, almost unbearable tension filled her as she waited.

"I think—" Jake whispered huskily as he paused "—that I'd better go read that contract first."

Heather's eyes flew open in astonishment as she felt her chin abruptly released. Hastily she covered her reaction, tilting her head proudly.

"You do that, Jake. I wouldn't want you getting involved in something you can't handle!" And a little too loudly, she closed the door in his face.

2

SHE LOOKED GOOD sitting there on the terrace, Jake decided the next morning as he approached the private garden area where the Strands customarily took breakfast. The warm morning sunlight gleamed on the neat sweep of her golden-brown hair, making him wish he'd followed through on the temptation to touch it last night.

Heather was wearing cream-colored cotton pants, pleated and full at the top, narrow at the ankle. The style emphasized in a chic way the intriguing roundness of her derriere and the delicacy of her anklebones. A blouse of the same color with a small collar and pleated sleeves gave Heather a rakish look that suited her.

Whatever she lacked in outright beauty she more than made up for in style and animation. It was no wonder people were instinctively attracted to her, Jake thought. Those lively hazel eyes could make you feel unique and very important. That surprisingly soft mouth curved readily into a smile of genuine warmth. However, there was more than a hint of assertiveness in the firm lines of chin and jaw, and that hint, coupled with her self-confidence, was all the warning Jake needed. Heather might have been a handful when she was a teenager, but that was nothing compared to what she would be now if she was seriously thwarted.

Unconsciously Jake drew a determined breath and stepped forward to greet Paul and Ruth Strand and their daughter. His fingers locked tightly around the contract in his hand.

Heather glanced up and set down her glass of orange juice as she caught sight of Jake's approaching figure. He crossed the brick terrace with easy familiarity. She had learned during the past two weeks just how very much at home Jake was with her parents, but occasionally when she saw a fresh manifestation of that ease something in her bristled. She should know by now that he often came to share coffee with Paul and Ruth, but this morning she instinctively resisted the idea of realizing just how much a part of the family he really was.

Then again, she decided with blunt self-honesty, perhaps that was one reason she was willing to marry him. A part of her longed to regain every foothold she'd ever had with her family. Marrying a man of whom they approved was one more way of cementing the new relationship.

"Good morning, Jake," Ruth Strand said warmly, reaching for the silver coffeepot and pouring the contents into the delicate English china cup. She added cream without bothering to inquire. She'd obviously poured coffee for Jake frequently.

"Good morning, Ruth. Paul." Jake nodded at both senior Strands and then strode directly to the chair in which Heather sat and leaned over with a casual possessiveness to kiss her firmly on her surprised mouth.

The decidedly familiar caress came as a shock to Heather. Before she had time to assimilate the hard feel of his mouth on hers, he had withdrawn to take the empty chair at the round table. A crinkle of paper made her glance down at her lap where he had left the contract he'd been carrying. When she glanced up questioningly, Jake merely smiled his strange half-amused smile.

"I read it last night. It made interesting bedtime reading."

"Did it?" she asked aloofly, aware of her parents' interest. They knew nothing about the prenuptial agreement but were obviously quite pleased at the familiarity between their daughter and Jake Cavender.

"I only made one small change," Jake went on, lifting the white napkin off the bread basket to fish around inside for a croissant. "Other than that everything looks in order. I went ahead and signed."

Heather's brows came together in concentration as she hastily began to flip through the contract. Ignoring her, Jake and her parents immediately fell to discussing the weather.

"The thunderstorms have been rather heavy this year," Paul remarked. "Worst I can remember in quite a while. Did you and Heather get caught in that big one last night?" A large man, capable of great charm or great wrath, Paul Strand had enjoyed his years as a hotelier. Still a handsome man, he was regally bald, and there was a certain heaviness around the jawline. But he was in excellent shape physically, played golf several times a week. He had passed along to his daughter the intelligent hazel eyes and the energetic decisive

temperament. It was very pleasant these days for
Heather to bask in the warmth of his approval. There
had been too many years when she'd been unable to
enjoy that hearty pleasure.

Her mother, Ruth, had been the source of Heather's
bronzed hair. On Ruth it was grayed in a most attractive fashion, however, and she wore it in a short,
charmingly windswept style. Both of Heather's sisters
had inherited their mother's vivid blue eyes and her
delicate bone structure. Liz and Ann, married and living nearby, were younger carbon copies of their petite
mother. Heather was taller, firmer and not as pretty as
Liz and Ann. The eldest daughter had inherited, in
short, a great deal from her father.

"We were safely tucked away eating dinner and discussing the, uh, business of our marriage when last
night's storm hit," Jake assured Paul. "Would you pass
the jam, please, Ruth?"

"Of course, dear." Ruth handed him the tiny silver
jam pot with a fond glance. "Now that everything's
settled I can't wait to start planning the actual ceremony. I was thinking of having the reception here in the
gardens. What do you think, Heather?"

Heather only half heard her mother's question. She
had just flipped back to the last page of the contract and
found Jake's one "small" change. Heavily lined out was
the paragraph regarding the physical side of the proposed marriage.

"Heather? Did you hear me, dear? I was thinking of
having the reception right here. Your father and I have
always loved this terrace. It would be far enough away
from the main lodge so that the hotel guests wouldn't

be affected. We could set up a bar along the brick wall and . . . Heather?"

"Yes, Mother?" Heather's head came up finally, but though she obediently responded to her parent, her narrowed gaze was focused tightly on Jake.

"I was talking about the wedding plans. Really, dear, you shouldn't get involved with the business of running Hacienda Strand until after your marriage. You know your father and Jake have tried to keep you away from the office until everything is settled. You've been working so hard in San Francisco. You need to take the next couple of weeks off and enjoy yourself. Think of all the fun you'll have planning your wedding."

"Fun?" Heather wrenched her eyes away from Jake who seemed patiently oblivious to the message in the hazel gaze. "Weddings aren't supposed to be fun, Mother. At least not for the bride and groom," she said. "Weddings are an ancient way of formalizing a contract between two people. The only important people at a wedding are the guests. They're the witnesses to the contract. It's a romantic misconception to think that the bride and groom should enjoy themselves. After all, it's primarily a business arrangement that's being concluded, isn't it?"

As soon as the words were out of her mouth, Heather could have kicked herself. The chagrined expression on her mother's soft face was reproach enough. It didn't take Paul Strand's uneasy disapproval to make Heather realize she'd made a mistake. She didn't often make such mistakes these days. But something about the quietly arrogant manner in which Jake had modified the prenuptial agreement had caught her on the raw.

She had spoken out of irritation that should have been directed at him, not at her parents.

It was Jake who gave her the opening she needed to recover.

"Can't I even have a glass of champagne and some cake at my own wedding?" he complained around a bite of flaky croissant. "Are you going to spoil all my fun?"

Heather turned to stare at him. His expression of wounded disappointment was so reminiscent of a young boy who has just been told he can't have any cake on his birthday that she couldn't resist: "One glass of champagne and half a slice of cake," Heather conceded with mock reluctance, as if she was doing him a tremendous favor. "Whether or not you'll get more will depend on how well you behave."

"Ouch!" Paul Strand grinned at the younger man as Ruth broke into what sounded like relieved laughter. "I hope you realize you're marrying a rather strong-willed female."

"Takes after her father, I'm told," Jake said nodding. "But I'm as much a victim of her charm as everyone else around here, so I suppose I will let her lead me to the altar regardless of whether or not she lets me have any cake and eat it, too."

"If I let you have cake, you're going to have to compromise on a few other issues." Heather got to her feet and waved the contract at him. "If you'll excuse me, I think I'll go have a look at the kitchens. I promised myself a tour of them today and all this talk about food has whetted my appetite to speak to the chef and his staff."

"Heather, as your mother just told you there's no need for you to rush around before the wedding. There will be plenty of time to get to know Hacienda Strand again after the honeymoon." Paul frowned at Jake. "Won't there?"

"All the time in the world," Jake agreed equably, polishing off his croissant. "On the other hand, perhaps a tour of the kitchens would keep her out of trouble. I saw her eyeing a motorcycle one of the busboys just bought."

"A motorcycle!" Ruth looked momentarily stricken.

Heather saw the shadow of remembered anguish that passed in her mother's eyes and instantly paused beside the other woman to drop a quick affectionate kiss on her cheek.

"I'm a businesswoman these days, remember? Soon to be married to a solid respectable man. I don't do wild and reckless things anymore," she assured Ruth with gentle humor. "I'm home."

The last two words hung in the air for a moment and then Ruth Strand smiled lovingly and caught her daughter's hand in her own. "Yes, you're home, aren't you? A fully grown woman, a successful businessperson in her own right and about to be married to a wonderful man. What could be more perfect?"

"Jake's turning red," Paul Strand interrupted lightly. "All this talk about his wonderfulness is going to his head. Better go on to the kitchens and have that tour, honey."

"Don't worry about my ego," Jake growled as he took Heather's arm. "Solid respectability has never been much of a compliment. I'm not likely to let such praise from my future wife go to my head."

"Oh, but it's not just your respectability that I admire," Heather shot back guilelessly. "I'm vastly impressed with your business talents, as well."

"That certainly reassures me," he said dryly. "Come on. Let's go tour the kitchens before you sweep me off my feet entirely."

Paul Strand's satisfied remark as Heather left the terrace on Jake's arm followed them down the steps. "I told you they were going to make a terrific team, Ruth."

Beside her, Jake's mouth twisted in amusement. "I think he means a perfect management team," he murmured so that only Heather could hear. "What do you think?"

"That he might be right. So long as both members of the team remember which of them is ultimately in charge." Heather kept her words light but gave the remark a definite emphasis that could not go unnoticed.

"Is that the main reason you came home, Heather? So that you could be in charge of the family hotel?" As they walked through the lush grounds, Jake glanced around at the elegantly designed complex. The main lodge, as well as the outlying cottages and facilities, were all done in a warm Spanish style. Heavy white stuccoed walls were accented with dark beams and graciously arched windows. The grounds were an oasis in the Tucson desert, rich and green from years of meticulous care. Crushed-gravel walks wandered randomly throughout the hotel gardens and there were guests out enjoying them in the fresh morning.

It was not the peak season for the Hacienda Strand. That would come in winter and spring when the freezing winds and blankets of snow up north drove those who could afford it to take a vacation in the balmy Arizona climate. It was a good time to be planning a wedding and learning the ropes of running the hotel, Heather had decided. By the time the busy season approached she would be completely settled in her new life.

"I didn't come home just to run the place," Heather informed him evenly. "I could have had that opportunity at more than one hotel in California. I'm here because . . . because I'm ready to be here."

"And you weren't ready when you were eighteen, is that what you're saying?"

"That's right." She shook the contract in her hand, anxious to change the subject before he could probe too deeply. "Jake, about that clause you marked out. I think we should discuss it immediately and come to terms."

"What terms?" he asked flatly. "I agreed to every other clause in the contract, including the one that stipulates that if the marriage is dissolved both of us will leave with only that which was our own property before the wedding. I agreed that anything bought by both of us during the term of the marriage would be split fifty-fifty at the time of a divorce. And I went along with the part that said anything bought independently during the marriage remained the private property of the party that made the purchase should the marriage be dissolved. Having agreed to all that, I can't see you have any cause to complain just because I crossed out one small clause."

"A rather important small clause!"

He glanced down at her. "You think a nice solid respectable man like me is going to throw himself on his bride on the wedding night and demand his rights? You think I'd rape you, Heather?"

She flinched and turned her head. "Of course not."

"Then why do you need that clause about giving the marriage six months before deciding whether or not to take matters beyond the platonic level?" he asked.

"I wanted to give our relationship time to grow and develop. You and I barely know each other, Jake. On the few occasions when I've been back to visit my parents during the past couple of years, you and I have met and talked on only a very casual basis, and even those times were the result of my mother's rather obvious matchmaking. If all goes according to schedule we'll be married at the end of the month. Four weeks is hardly long enough to rebuild the relationship with my parents, let alone develop one with you. We need time before we carry this marriage beyond the business level and that clause was a way of assuring us both time. Knowing that there won't be any pressure to consummate the marriage in the next six months will take a burden off both our shoulders."

"Thanks, but I think I can handle the strain of making love to my wife," he replied sardonically. "Granted, not every man could bear such a burden, but when duty calls. . . ."

"This is not a joking matter!" she told him tartly.

His mouth tightened. "I'm not joking, Heather. When you proposed to me last week I accepted on the assumption that the marriage would be a real one. As you took such pains to point out last night, you and I have a lot to offer each other. But I have no interest in contracting a purely business arrangement. I want a real marriage."

"Oh, it will be real, all right. My mother's got a guest list with nearly two hundred names on it and my father has told every one of his golfing buddies that he's going to have three different brands of champagne at the reception plus a full bar. My sisters called yesterday to say they've found the perfect gown and that my little nephew is going to be the ring bearer. Believe me, that sort of pomp and circumstance makes everything very real!"

Jake stopped and put his hands on her shoulders, turning her to face him. Something softened in his expression. "You're getting nervous, aren't you?"

"I am not nervous." She tried to twist out from under the strong grip of his fingers and found it impossible to move. In rigid annoyance she stood quite still and lifted her chin challengingly.

"Are you sure you're not starting to wonder just what you've gotten yourself into by coming back to Tucson to play the role of the returning prodigal daughter?" Jake went on gently.

"I'm not playing any role. I'm home, Jake, because this is where I want to be. This desert and those beautiful mountains are in my blood. They've always been a part of me. Just as my family is a part of me and just as the Hacienda Strand is a part of me. I had to leave at eighteen or all these things that are a part of me would have smothered me. I didn't know which battles were worth waging and which simply weren't important. I had to rebel against almost everything because I didn't know which factors would control me and which I could control. I could not accept my father's money then because I had to prove I could earn my own. I couldn't accept Hacienda Strand then because I had to prove I deserved to be in charge of it. I couldn't accept the love of my family because I didn't know how to keep my family from controlling me."

"But now you can handle it all? Is that what you're saying?"

"I'm a woman now, not a child. I've proven myself."

"And you know which battles are worth fighting."

"Yes."

Jake regarded her intently. "Heather, this battle over the clause I crossed out of the contract is not worth fighting."

"And if I happen to believe differently?"

"Then I shall have to decline your kind offer." He smiled rather wistfully. "You're not the only one who's come home, Heather. The Hacienda Strand is my home now, too. Your parents have made me feel almost like a part of the family. Your father trusts me completely. Your mother thinks I'm going to make you an excellent husband. You yourself plan to work with me day in and day out running the Hacienda. And unless you plan on running off again with some punk on a motorcycle, we're committed, you and I. We're in this together for the duration. But if I'm going to link my life and my career with yours then I want a full, 100 percent commitment. I don't want a ridiculous sham of a marriage. I want the real thing. Hearth, home and family. In exchange for agreeing to all of your terms, I expect you to agree to mine."

Heather caught her breath, suddenly fiercely aware of the strength in his hands and the unyielding intensity of his eyes. The morning sun beat warmly down on the gardens, coaxing an earthy scent from the rain-moistened ground. That scent seemed to combine with Jake's clean masculine essence, making her overwhelmingly conscious of him in a way she instinctively knew was dangerous. It was difficult to marshal her thoughts into logical arguments.

There were many things she could have said; should have said. She ought to have pointed out that his career at the Hacienda could be terminated at any time by her. She could have argued that she hadn't actually ruled out intimacy in the marriage; merely postponed the decision. She might have stressed her refusal to be pushed beyond certain limits. After all, returning prodigals were willing to be cooperative up to a point, but only up to a point.

Instead she heard herself say crisply, "We'll talk about it later. I'm late for that tour of the kitchens and it's been my experience that first-class chefs hate to be kept waiting."

"We'll talk about it now, Heather. This is my future as well as your own we're discussing. I want this aspect of it settled."

His stubbornness threatened to trigger her carefully buried instinct to rebel. With an extreme effort of will, Heather reminded herself that she had nothing serious against which to rebel. She was in charge here. It was up to her how much territory she decided to yield.

"You're the one who's nervous, aren't you?" she challenged softly. "It's your future here at the Hacienda that's on the line, not mine. Well, I can understand that. After all, you're not a full-fledged member of my family. Only marrying me can give you that status."

"Let's just say I'm willing to work hard to get the feeling of having roots and a family and a place to call home. All the things you once threw away so casually and have come back to claim."

"I didn't realize marrying me was going to be such hard work!"

"I'm beginning to think it's going to be the hardest job I've ever undertaken." But he was smiling again and Heather was beginning to realize just how much she liked that strange little half smile.

"Even more of a reason not to add the extra burden of doing your husbandly duty in bed!" she retorted briskly.

He sobered. "Heather, I'm not going to rush you into giving me anything you're not prepared to give. All I'm asking is that we don't set deadlines on something as private and personal as this aspect of our marriage. You have my word I won't demand my so-called rights. In return I'd like yours that you'll let things happen naturally without restrictions and contractual clauses. Is that too much to request?"

She stared up at him wonderingly, startled by the genuine honesty in his voice. He was so close, so intent and quietly insistent that she didn't know how to handle the situation. She needed time.

"Jake—"

Heather got no further in her demand. Jake lowered his head, a smoky quality invading the gray depths of his eyes, and the next thing Heather knew her mouth was being slowly and deliberately consumed by his.

His kiss wasn't quite what she had expected. For one thing she certainly hadn't anticipated this degree of controlled hunger. Oddly dazed by the experience, she unconsciously sank her fingertips into the fabric of the tailored, pin-striped shirt he wore. His mouth moved on hers, exploring, tasting, learning the feel of her in incredibly intimate fashion.

She felt his hands slide around her waist to find the gentle curve at the base of her spine. Then he applied a steady pressure, urging her against his thighs. It was a small shock to her body to learn the promise of heat and hardness that awaited her there. Her lips parted in a low moan of uncertainty; a moan that was silenced as his tongue luxuriously invaded her mouth.

Heather clung to him, her body vibrantly aware of the gathering warmth of both the day and the man who held her. Her instincts responded to both and her fingertips curved around his broad shoulders in a small gesture of budding excitement. He wanted her. And the flickering uncoiling sensation in the deepest places of her body warned Heather that Jake could make her want him.

Slowly, with infinite reluctance Jake lifted his head. He continued to hold her molded to the length of his lean body, and the gray smoke of his gaze reflected the lingering, heavily restrained desire in him.

"Don't fight it, Heather. There's no reason we shouldn't want each other, is there?" he murmured with soft male persuasion. "After all, we're going to be married."

Heather tried to speak, swallowed and tried again. "No, there's no reason. It's just that I . . . we, well, we hardly know each other and there's been so little time." She was stumbling over the words, and the knowledge both alarmed and irritated her. After all, she was nearly thirty years old with several years' experience in handling all kinds of males. She had dealt with them as friends, co-workers, employers and employees.

But all things considered, she hadn't dealt with them very often as lovers.

"Heather, we don't need that clause in the contract. Trust me this much, will you? A little trust is a valuable ingredient in any kind of relationship, marriage or business."

"You won't rush me?"

"I won't rush you."

"You won't make demands?"

"I won't make demands."

"You won't sulk or argue or give me the silent treatment if I take my time deciding what I want?"

"I can guarantee I won't sulk." There was amusement in his lightening expression.

Heather responded to it, her lips curving in an equally humorous smile. "Then I suppose we can keep that part of the contract on a verbal agreement basis," she declared judiciously.

"You drive a hard bargain, lady."

"My father was an excellent teacher." Heather pulled free of his light embrace and started down the path toward the kitchens. When he fell into step beside her, slowing his long gliding stride to match hers, she knew a pleasant sense of having resolved an uneasy issue.

"Call it a compromise, Heather," Jake suggested gently.

"Mother has been lecturing me all week on the necessity of compromising in marriage," Heather admitted with a tiny grin.

"You've been very patient with Ruth's attempts to organize our wedding. It means a lot to her."

"I know."

"Are you trying to make up for the way you ran off eleven years ago?"

"Perhaps."

Jake considered that in silence as they walked through the side doors of the gleaming kitchens of the Hacienda Strand. Whatever he would have said in response was lost as they confronted the scene of energetic, highly skilled activity that greeted them. The kitchens had been redone two years previously and as a result they were a model of stainless-steel efficiency and cleanliness. Heather remembered this place as a refuge in her childhood. Here she had been able to come after school for a chocolate-chip cookie and a glass of milk. It was here, too, where she could make herself scarce whenever her father was annoyed with her. For some reason he never thought to come looking in the kitchens. And it had been here where she had found someone to teach her how to ride a motorcycle that last year in high school.

"Miss Strand! You made it. We've been looking forward to your visit. Come on in, come on in."

"Hello, Julian," Heather said with a smile as the robust chef, Julian Richards, came toward them through the scurrying staff like a large ocean liner coming into port. "After those croissants this morning you couldn't have kept me away. I would never have believed I could find anything like them outside San Francisco. And the fettuccine with anchovy sauce the other evening was absolutely superb. I would have returned to Tucson years ago if I'd known you had been added to the staff."

The middle-aged chef beamed under the lavish praise and was about to respond when he appeared to notice that Heather was not alone. "Ah, Mr. Cavender. I'm pleased that you decided to come along on the tour. We don't see very much of you in the kitchens." There was both respect and reproach in the words.

Heather heard the warmth fade from the chef's voice as he turned to greet Jake. It wasn't that he became less gracious, but he was definitely more wary and more distant.

This wasn't the first time during the past two weeks Heather had seen this reaction from members of the staff when they confronted Jake Cavender. They seemed a little uncertain of him, as if they were conscious of walking on crystal eggs around him. There was definitely respect in their manner, but none of the easy relations most of the staff enjoyed with the more jovial Paul Strand. That cordiality and warmth was rapidly being extended to his daughter, however. It had added greatly to Heather's enjoyable sense of homecoming.

"None of the guests have been complaining," Jake said quietly, "so I saw no reason to interfere."

Julian shrugged with Gallic resignation although Heather knew the man had no French ancestry. She'd asked him specifically the night he'd served her a magnificent dish of mussels in saffron sauce. He'd been thrilled that she had concluded he must have learned his cooking skills at the knee of a French mother.

"Well, we hope you, Miss Strand, will not choose to show up in the kitchens only when something goes wrong," Julian declared regally and gallantly offered his arm to escort her into the pastry section. "Carlos, give Miss Strand a sample of that shortbread you made this morning."

The young man wielding a rolling pin paused with a grin and handed Heather a sample of the still-warm shortbread.

"Believe me, if I can be guaranteed a bite or two of this sort of thing every time I visit, you will have to shoo me away from your doors." Aware of Jake's dark silent presence trailing along behind her, Heather took half the rich buttery cookie and turned on impulse to feed the other half to him.

He looked somewhat surprised at the offering but hesitated only a fraction of a second before accepting it. He didn't politely extend his hand for it, however. Heather was a little disconcerted to find herself popping the morsel between his strong white teeth. The unexpected intimacy of the small action brought a slight flush to Heather's cheeks.

When she hurriedly swung around to continue the tour she found a number of grins being quickly concealed. Even Julian appeared both astonished and amused. The staff, Heather presumed, was not accustomed to seeing the remote financial wizard of Hacienda Strand being fed shortbread in such a casual manner. Heather had to stifle a grin of her own as Jake dutifully followed her and her escort into the section where fresh vegetables were being washed.

Heather listened attentively and sampled cheerfully until, with a faintly apologetic air, Julian led her toward a grill on which several hamburgers were about to be cooked.

"For the children, you understand. Many of the guests here at the Hacienda bring their kids and all the young ones want are hamburgers. Even at ten-thirty in the morning! This order has just come in from the pool area."

"Of course," Heather said laughing. "Children work up a healthy appetite swimming." She stepped toward the grill with easy familiarity. "Personally I'll always have a warm spot in my heart for hamburgers. I owe them a great deal, you see. It's been a few years since I cooked them in quantity, though. I wonder if I still have the knack. Let me see that spatula."

"Miss Strand, you'll get all greasy," Julian protested as she reached for the stack of hamburger patties separated by thin sheets of paper.

"I cannot believe you would buy fatty meat, Julian. Now, we can't forget the buns. Jake, wash your hands over there and do the buns."

There was a startled silence behind Heather and it wasn't just Jake who was astounded. The entire staff was suddenly too quiet and too tense. Heather glanced around.

"Jake? Aren't you going to help me? There are a lot of hungry kids out by that pool. Mustn't have the guests starving."

He stared at her while beside him Julian Richards moved restlessly. The chef clearly was not sure how to handle matters at this point. Then, to everyone's carefully suppressed astonishment, Jake obediently went to a nearby sink and washed his hands.

"You'll have to explain the process," he said evenly as he came to stand beside Heather. "I've never done this before."

"Your education was definitely lacking. Use that little brush to slather the melted butter on the buns and then throw the little suckers on the grill behind the hamburgers. They'll all be ready at the same time—like magic. We're only dealing with eight burgers here. Heck, in a pinch I can handle almost five times that many."

"Your education, apparently, was more complete than mine." With careful strokes Jake began painting the buns a golden color with the melted butter. Then, wary of the splattering grill surface, he set them down in a neat row beyond the burgers. Behind him the kitchen staff watched in fascination.

A few minutes later the eight burgers were finished, neatly sandwiched into their buns and ready for delivery to the poolside. Chef Richards exhaled deeply.

"One thing is certain," he chuckled. "The two of you will never go hungry. You can always get jobs as short-order cooks somewhere. By the way," he went on more formally. "May I take this opportunity to extend the congratulations of my staff and myself. We were all very happy to learn of your forthcoming marriage."

"Thank you," Jake responded equally formally. His arm settled around Heather's narrow waist in a possessive manner.

"And thank you for the tour, Julian," Heather added quickly as Jake escorted her toward the door. "I'll be back."

"Anytime, Miss Strand. Anytime."

"As usual—" Jake murmured as they stepped out into the mounting heat of the summer day "—you've made another conquest. The kitchen staff is now yours to command."

"Actually, I thought you took commands fairly well yourself back there. Hard to believe you've never had to cook hamburger buns on a grill before."

"Your directions were very clear," he told her dryly.

"And you carried them out well. I'm beginning to think everyone around here may be right."

"About what?"

"About us making a good team."

Jake tugged her to a halt. "I've been telling you that all along."

"So you have. So has my father. And so has the rest of the family." Heather smiled. "And you're quite certain you won't mind working for a woman?"

He hesitated, as if choosing his words with care. "I think I can work *with* you, Heather."

She smiled brilliantly. "I really do make a very good boss, if I do say so myself."

"And what kind of wife will you make?"

She shrugged fatalistically. "Who knows? I've never had any experience. What are your qualifications as a husband?"

Jake moved his head in a slow negative, the brackets hard on either side of his mouth. "My direct experience is quite limited. I was married once, Heather. A long time ago. We were both very young, very immature and very broke. I think we thought marriage would somehow cure all that. It was a romantic fantasy that didn't last eighteen months. At the end of that time we were still young and broke but perhaps a little wiser."

Heather's eyes gentled as she remembered her own youthful passions and fantasies. "What happened, Jake?"

"She found someone else who could support her in the style to which she wanted to become accustomed." There was no bitterness in his words. "When she announced she wanted a divorce, my main feeling, I'm afraid, was one of relief. In the end it was the best answer for everyone. She got the security she needed and I had the freedom to spend every dime I could earn on an education. After I got my business degree I was too busy building a career to think about marriage. Or maybe I just never found anyone who seemed to want the same things I wanted. I don't know. I do know," he added with quiet emphasis, "that I am ready again for marriage, and this time I intend to make it work."

"You sound very certain of that."

"I've grown used to getting what I want out of life, Heather. Even if I have to get it the hard way. And I don't take failure easily."

She wasn't certain how to take that declaration. It was hardly a ringing vow of love. But, then, she wasn't interested in a marriage of fluff and fantasy. She wanted a working partner and Jake sounded as if he was willing to work, both for the Hacienda Strand and for the marriage.

"Well," she quipped, seeking a way to lighten the heavy direction of the conversation, "at least this time if we wind up married and broke we'll know we can do as Julian suggested and get jobs cooking hamburgers. We won't go hungry."

To her surprise he took the joking remarks seriously. "If that's what it takes, that's what we'll do."

Heather turned away with a small frown. Drive and determination were normally qualities she admired in others and had an abundance of herself. But in Jake Cavender those two attributes were overlaid with an intensity that occasionally sent uneasy chills down her spine.

3

ONE WEEK BEFORE the wedding Jake stood beside Paul Strand on the Strands' private garden terrace and watched Heather circulate through the crowd of beautifully dressed people her mother had invited. The party was in honor of the engaged couple but somehow it seemed to have turned into Heather's party.

Colorful Japanese lanterns cast an appealing glow over the gathering. The afternoon thunderstorms had come and gone, removing temporarily at least, some of the typical August mugginess. Glasses and ice clinked as the guests cheerfully downed Paul Strand's expensive liquor along with Julian Richards's beautiful canapés.

Jake sipped meditatively at his Scotch and reminded himself for what must surely have been the hundredth time that evening, that in another week he would be married to the vivid creature across the room.

Dressed in a deceptively simple jewel-toned silk gown that plunged rather daringly in back and was demurely high in front, her hair polished and sleek, Heather had taken over the party from the moment it had begun. Jake caught glimpses of her smiling animated features as she charmed her way through the evening, and something fierce tugged at his insides.

He wanted her. He'd been wanting her for three weeks. It seemed like forever.

For a moment he entertained a brief satisfying fantasy of cornering her at the party, throwing her over his shoulder and carrying her off into the night. Three weeks of restraint shouldn't have been affecting him so much, he told himself wryly. He was a man, not a boy. He took another swallow of the Scotch and gazed broodingly at his future bride. Heather was busy coaxing the normally shy Cecil Winthrop into lively conversation.

"Never saw Cecil loosen up so much at a party before," Paul Strand observed humorously. He slicked back the fawn-colored cuff of his well-tailored sport coat and glanced at his watch. "Normally he claims he has to be in bed by ten and here it is going on eleven."

"He's captivated by Heather. Just like everyone else here tonight."

"I told you she would make the perfect hostess for the Hacienda, didn't I?" Paul grinned complacently as he glanced at the younger man. "With your brains and her natural ability to handle people, the two of you are going to make this hotel the finest in Arizona."

"How did you know she was going to be so good with people, Paul? You and Ruth have told me for two years that she nearly drove you crazy before she left home."

"Ah, but even when she was driving us crazy she could twist anyone on the staff around her little finger. I'd yell at her for going swimming in front of the guests in a bikini that was two sizes too small, and the next thing I knew she was being cosseted in the kitchens, stuffing herself with cookies and soda pop while the waiters and the cooks commiserated with her. I always knew she had the brains and the willpower to make something of herself, and it used to drive me to distraction to see her rely on easy charm to get what she wanted."

"She seems to have developed both brains and willpower during the last few years," Jake observed. "She'd made quite a name for herself in hotel management circles before she told you she was coming home. You don't get her kind of reputation on charm alone."

Paul chuckled. "I know. Actually, she's a great deal more lethal now than she was when she was a kid."

"Charm and intelligence can be a dangerous combination," Jake agreed.

"And you, Jake, are just the man to handle that combination. Why else do you think I've been pushing this marriage? The two of you are going to make a perfect team."

"I think," Jake muttered a little gruffly, "that after we're officially a 'team' I'm going to have her give that dress to the Salvation Army."

Paul grinned. "It's cut a little low in the back, I'll admit. Ruth did try to say something about it before the party, but these days my daughter does what she wants. Fortunately for all concerned most of the things she seems to want now are what the rest of us want for her. But occasionally she puts her foot down. The difference now is that she draws the line in a very calm firm manner instead of throwing a tantrum. She's a woman."

And she's going to be my woman, Jake told himself, trying to squelch the reckless excitement that thought brought. One more week.

"Oh, there you are, Dad!" Liz Strand, the youngest of the Strand daughters, appeared in front of Jake and Paul. "Isn't it a wonderful party?" Her lovely face was alight with pleasure. "Of course, everyone came to see the prodigal daughter but they're staying because they're having such a wonderful time. Heather's got them all eating out of the palm of her hand. Isn't it fun?"

"Great fun," Paul agreed on a laugh. "Where's Ann?"

"Over there with her husband. I was just on my way to get some more of those luscious canapés Julian fixed. He really pulled out all the stops for this party, didn't he?"

"Heather's got him thinking he's the greatest chef to come along since the guy who invented the cheese soufflé," Jake grumbled.

Liz grinned. "Well, since it was your idea to hire Julian two years ago, I should think you'd be pleased he's so charmed by my sister. After all, now that he's given the Hacienda Strand such a good reputation for fine dining, you'd hate to have him lured off by a competitor."

"She's got a point," Paul agreed cheerfully. "Your safest bet is to have Julian under Heather's spell. Wouldn't want to lose him."

"No. I wouldn't want to lose him. Excuse me," Jake said a little grimly, "but I do appear to have lost track of my fiancée. I'd better go find her." With a nod to Liz and Paul, Jake waded determinedly into the crowd.

Since moving to the sunbelt he had learned to dress in the casual Arizona style, but even though he wore a light-colored sport coat and an open-necked shirt, something about the way he wore his clothes tonight set him a little apart from the other men. The vaguely remote quality that was so much a factor in his nature simply refused to yield to the easygoing effects of the clothing. The people around him responded in kind. They nodded in a friendly manner, spoke respectfully, but there was a faint wariness in them. No one was quite sure how to take Jake Cavender.

That situation changed, however, when he finally located Heather and moved to take his place at her side. In the course of responding to Heather's charm, people found themselves feeling more at ease with Jake, too.

"Good evening, Cavender," Cecil Winthrop greeted him in a far more jovial manner than usual as Jake handed Heather the glass of Chenin Blanc he'd procured en route.

Jake nodded politely. He didn't fool himself for a minute. Winthrop was generally not this friendly and his cordiality tonight was strictly because of Heather. "Hello, Cecil. I'm glad to see you're enjoying yourself."

Heather smiled brilliantly. "Cecil and I were just discussing the time I used his land to practice riding my motorcycle. I forgot to ask Cecil's permission." She shook her head in rueful apology. "It was just that your land was so terribly convenient, Cecil. I'm not even sure where the Hacienda Strand's land ends and yours begins!"

"Jake knows, don't you, my boy?" Cecil asked. One bushy gray brow arched behind his wire-frame glasses.

"I admit I've studied the matter," Jake replied uncomfortably. This was the last thing he wanted to discuss tonight. After the marriage would be a much better time.

But Heather was already turning a curious face toward him. "Am I missing something here?"

"Just a small matter of business," Jake assured her quickly. "Nothing to discuss at the moment."

"Your husband-to-be has some plans for all that acreage I've got that borders the Hacienda Strand property," Cecil confided cheerfully to Heather. "He and I have discussed the matter from time to time."

"I see." Heather pinned Jake with a glance. "What plans?"

Jake hid his irritation at having the subject brought up. "I had some thoughts of using that land to put in a private golf course for the Hacienda," he told her brusquely.

"You had some thoughts? What's my father's opinion?"

"Heather, we'll discuss this later." Taking her arm very firmly, Jake nodded at Cecil Winthrop. "Sorry to drag her away, Cecil, but Paul's been trying to find her all evening. Please excuse us."

"Of course, of course. Mustn't monopolize the guest of honor," Cecil agreed with a gracious wave. He smiled again at Heather.

Heather managed an unconcerned smile in return but as soon as they were out of earshot she deliberately disengaged her arm. "What in the world was that all about?" she demanded in a low voice, nodding pleasantly at the guests they were passing.

"Just a little business matter. There will be plenty of time to talk about it later."

"You want to put in a private golf course for the Hacienda guests?"

"I thought it would be a great drawing card for the hotel. Everyone comes to Tucson to play golf in the winter." Jake sighed, knowing there was no way around the discussion now that Heather was onto the subject.

"But our guests have playing privileges at most of the major courses in the area. I don't see that we need to provide our own. What did my father say when you came up with the idea?"

"Heather, we'll talk about this later. Tonight you're supposed to be socializing, remember? Your family doesn't want you being concerned with business until after the honeymoon."

"I know," she said wryly. "It's been getting rather annoying. Dad won't even talk about the details of turning over the reins to me. Every time I bring up the subject he just goes on and on about what a fine management team you and I will make. So far I've put up with everyone's efforts to keep me away from business until after the wedding, but frankly I'm beginning to chomp at the bit. I can't wait to step into my new role. Oh, Jake, I love this place so much and it's been a dream of mine so long to come back and assume Dad's position. After all these years it feels good to return to the family business. There's a sense of heritage and tradition about it. I've missed that feeling in California."

Jake's face was stony. "There will be plenty of time to learn your new role after the wedding, Heather. Just be patient. You're making your family very happy by going along with all this, you know." He nodded at the crowd around them.

"And you're wondering when the party's finally going to end, aren't you, Jake?" she teased lightly.

"Socializing isn't my forte."

"I've noticed. Cheer up. Everyone will probably start leaving in another hour. Let's go see if there are any more of Julian's goodies left."

It was another hour and a half before the first guests started to leave; two hours before everyone had departed. But eventually Jake was able to pry Heather away from an in-depth postmortem of the successful event with her mother.

As they stepped out on the path that led to Heather's private cottage, he had a few thoughts about persuading her to come to his place instead. When he had arrived two years ago Paul had told him to take his pick of the graciously designed cottages. He'd chosen the one-bedroom style that had the charm of a modern adobe look. Heather, to date, had only stepped foot inside on two occasions: once to ask him to join her for a swim and once to bring him an invitation from her mother to join the Strands for cocktails before dinner. On neither occasion had she stayed more than a few minutes.

"Would you like to go to my place for a nightcap?" Jake tried carefully. The last thing he wanted to do at this stage was make her feel any sexual pressure. He'd gone far enough by crossing that six-month clause out of the contract. He'd been watching every move he made since then, allowing himself only casual kisses of greeting and a few rationed kisses of farewell at her door when he took her home at night. He knew he couldn't risk alarming her in any way.

Only a week to go.

"All right."

Her ready agreement took him by surprise. Perhaps he should have tried the invitation before. Jake felt a surge of eagerness. It was just barely possible she was going to accept the sensual attraction between them without any fuss. It would make things a hell of a lot simpler if she did. Firmly he guided her onto another path; one that led in the direction of his cottage.

"You were the queen of the evening," he said after a moment of silence. "Your parents were very proud of you. Liz and Ann were delighted. They got a kick out of the way you charmed the socks off everyone in sight."

Beside him Heather exhaled softly. "Everyone who showed up tonight did so for two reasons. One, they like my parents and wouldn't want to offend them, and two, they wanted to see how I'd turned out." Her tone was dry but not bitter. "Since I will be taking my place here in the business community, I had to put on a good performance."

"I don't think it was all a performance. You're in your element dealing with people, Heather. It comes naturally to you. You make them feel at ease, get them to talk. That's a valuable talent. I wish I had some of it."

"From the way my father talks about you, your own talents in finance and business administration more than make up for any lack of social skills you feel you have."

"Very diplomatic," he approved. "Will it bother you, Heather?"

"Will what bother me?"

"Being married to a man who's not as at ease with people as you are?"

He watched her consider the question, her face drawn in surprisingly contemplative lines. "No. To tell you the truth, I think the combination of two people who were overly social might be a bit much."

"Brains as well as charm," he murmured, silently acknowledging that her answer came as something of a relief.

"Was that a compliment?" she asked lightly.

"It was an observation your father made earlier this evening."

"Ah, my father." She nodded, pleased. "He's satisfied with the way I turned out, isn't he, Jake?"

"Very." Wisely he decided not to add that he himself was pleased. She might find the remark patronizing. Hell, he was sure trying to watch his footwork these days. Trying to be so careful, so restrained. It was a strain, to say the least. Unable to resist, Jake put his hand on Heather's waist, seeking the feel of her silky warm skin where it was bared by the plunging cut of the gown in back. She didn't move away.

They walked the rest of the way to his place in a companionable silence. The warm night enveloped them and the scent of the gardens was rich and enticing. Almost as tantalizing as the scent of the woman beside him, Jake thought. His fingers moved almost unconsciously on her back, tracing the beautiful line of her spine to the point where it disappeared beneath the fabric. Below that the womanly flare of her thighs beckoned. It required an effort of will not to let his hand stray inside the jewel-colored silk.

"I have some cognac," Jake began as he unlocked the front door and ushered her inside.

"That sounds delightful. Good heavens, I'm exhausted." With a delicately stifled yawn Heather dropped down in the black leather love seat that faced the fireplace. The hearth had been filled for the summer with dried flowers. It was nothing unique. The same maids who put the flowers on Jake's hearth had put them on all the cottage hearths. In the winter, wood would be provided for the nippy evenings. The advantages of living in a fine hotel.

Out of the corner of his eye Jake watched as Heather slipped off the incredibly high-heeled sandals she had been wearing all evening. The small faintly intimate act told him that she seemed to feel at home in his living room. A distinct flicker of satisfaction went through him as he poured the cognac and carried it across the Navaho rug.

Heather curled into the love seat, drawing her stockinged feet up under the hem of the silk dress. She reached for her glass, her hazel eyes meeting Jake's over the rim.

"To us," he said, gently tapping the side of his glass against hers.

"And to the Hacienda," she returned, sipping luxuriously. "It's been a long evening."

"Yes."

Jake sat down beside her, casually allowing his thigh to come in contact with her curving knee. The sensation stirred the already circulating restlessness in him but he craved the contact. *Like an addict*, he told himself grimly. *The more I'm around her the more I want of her.*

One more week. That thought seemed to be moving around inside his head tonight like loose shrapnel.

"Do you think going away for a few days to Santa Fe is really necessary, Jake? After all, we're already living in the kind of place people go for honeymoons," Heather joked softly.

He became still, gazing down into his cognac. This wasn't the first hesitation she had voiced about going away together. He wished he knew exactly what she was thinking. When he kissed her he could sense the beginnings of a response, but there was no way of knowing whether or not she'd allow herself to give in to that response next week or next month or six months from now. Heather Strand might once have been a creature of passionate impulse and spirited rebellion, but Jake knew she governed herself now with drive and determination. Her success in California and her cool poise could not have been bought with any other coin.

But he wouldn't have gotten where he was without the same type of currency. And for him the risk had been greater. There had been no rich welcoming family to fall back on in case he hadn't succeeded. He knew how to get what he wanted just as Heather did, but Jake told himself that, out of necessity, he'd learned to play a rougher game than any Heather had been forced to learn.

"Your family will expect us to go away for a while," he pointed out, seeking the most powerful argument he had at his disposal. Right now she seemed so anxious to please her family. Would she ever be equally anxious to please him? "So will the staff."

"I suppose so." She lifted one shoulder languidly beneath the beautifully hued silk. "Well, I think I can tolerate Santa Fe for a few days," she added with a flash of amusement. "I've never seen a town so devoted to being quaint and cute in my life as Santa Fe, New Mexico. Except possibly Carmel, California. We can go through the galleries and take in some of the concerts. It might be a nice break for both of us before we come back here and get ready for the season."

Jake's head came up, his face momentarily expressing some of the annoyance and frustration he was unable to totally repress. "It's supposed to be a honeymoon, not a 'nice break.'"

"Jake—"

"Heather, I've told you I won't push you. But in return I expect you to let things happen naturally."

"*Naturally* to a man generally means jumping into bed at the first opportunity, doesn't it?"

She was teasing him, he thought. It was impossible to tell exactly what she was thinking. The only times he trusted his reading of her responses were those rare moments when he held her in his arms. The temptation to push past her barriers of self-confidence and poise welled up in him.

"Why are you fighting it, Heather?"

She didn't pretend to misunderstand. "Because there's something in you that I don't quite understand yet. Something I don't *know* about you. I can't explain it any more clearly than that. I just know I need time."

He brushed aside the impatience he felt and put out a hand to touch the side of her cheek. "There are things I don't know or understand yet about you, either. But I think if we are honest with each other on this level..." He set down his glass and leaned forward to brush his mouth lingeringly across hers. "I think if we are honest on this level," he continued in a voice that was thickening slightly, "the rest will follow."

He let his lips hover above hers, watching both emotion and intelligence flicker in her hazel eyes. She did want him, he told himself exultantly. All he had to do was find a way to release her from the bonds of restraint she had placed on herself. He wanted to free the passionate rebel that must still be locked inside her somewhere.

Deliberately he lowered his mouth again, delighting in the small tremor that went through her when he crushed her lips beneath his own. She tasted of sweet womanly promise and of cognac; of late-night warmth and barriers that were not quite so strong at this hour. And when he thrust his tongue past her teeth, Jake was certain he tasted the beginnings of passion.

Slowly he crowded against her, removing the glass from her hand without lifting his mouth from hers. Her fingertips came up to sink into the fabric of his jacket and when he groaned in response she slid her hands inside.

"Your fingers feel so good on me," he growled against her mouth. "So good."

"Oh, Jake...."

"Relax, honey. We're going to take this slow. Slow and soft." *But it will be thorough,* he vowed silently as the fierce desire stoked the fires that had been simmering in him all evening. It would be thorough; complete. And when it was over she would belong to him.

Holding her mouth gently captive he began to explore the alluring curve at the place where her throat and shoulder merged. There was an intriguing vulnerability about her there. At his touch she twisted a little, whether in invitation or reaction he couldn't be certain. But it felt good. The gentle curve of her breasts pressed against him and quite suddenly he was certain that the daring gown had no built-in bra.

But the lecture about her dress would have to come later. At the moment he was enjoying the garment too much. He moved more heavily against her, wanting to feel the length of her body under his. She seemed to sink obediently in the leather love seat, her softness accommodating the hard planes and angles of him.

Opening his mouth on hers, he invited her inside, and when her tongue hesitantly accepted the sensual invitation, Jake's pulse pounded in reaction. Reining in his impulse to shred the light silk of her dress, he carefully drew his hand down its surface to find the sweet roundness of her breast.

He heard the catch in her breath as he let his palm graze enticingly over the hardening nipple.

"You feel so good," he muttered. The urge to see the taut tantalizing curve he was caressing made him reach for the sleeve of the silk dress. It slipped down her arm with satisfying ease and a moment later Heather was naked to the waist.

Jake felt the abrupt hesitation in her and raised his head to meet her questioning, half-concealed gaze. "Do you like my touch, Heather?" He used his thumb very gently on the revealing nipple.

"Isn't it obvious what your touch is doing to me?"

"I'd like to hear you say it," he rasped, aware of the urgency in himself.

"Yes," she breathed throatily. "I like your touch." She wrapped her arms around his neck with abrupt demand, a low moan parting her lips as she pulled his head back down to hers.

His head spinning with anticipation and skyrocketing need, Jake buried his lips against her throat and caught the tip of one of her breasts between his thumb and forefinger. She flinched at the caress and he knew it was because she was rapidly becoming gloriously sensitized.

"If you're this sensitive up here," he growled, "I can't wait to find out how sensitive you are down here." He freed her breasts for a moment to trail his hand down to her waist and beyond.

"Jake! Oh, Jake. . . ." Her head arched back over his arm as he deliberately allowed the heat of his palm to blend with the heat of her body. The thin silk barrier of her dress could not shield either of them.

"My God, lady. You're going to drive me crazy. Feel what you're doing to me!" He moved his hips against her thigh, letting her know of the throbbing hardness in him. "I want you, Heather. I want you very badly."

"Jake, I—" Her small tongue emerged to dampen her parted lips as she struggled for words. "We can't. Not yet. Too soon. Much too soon."

"How can it be too soon when we want each other this much?" Intent on making her acutely aware of both him and her own building passions, Jake boldly inserted his legs between her thighs, crushing the silk upward into the warm juncture of her body. The action bared the creamy softness of her upper thighs and he traced a small erotic pattern on the inside of her leg. She gasped and shifted beneath him.

"Jake, you promised you wouldn't rush me," she managed tightly.

"We have the rest of the night. No rush. I swear."

"No, Jake."

He felt her willpower as it began to reassert itself over her growing passion. Felt it and respected it even while he longed to overwhelm it. He could do it, he told himself. He could kiss the protests back into her throat, pull away the crumpled silk dress and take her. She would respond. She had to respond eventually. All that passion buried in her would surge to the surface if he could get past the barriers of her uncertainty. Even now her skin was hot and moist to the touch. A little longer...

"I mean it, Jake. Please let me go." She spoke as if she really expected no opposition. She sounded as if she knew she only had to be firm and make him back off. She had complete confidence in her ability to make him act the role of a gentleman.

The knowledge that she was right; that he would be bound by her decisions tonight was savagely frustrating.

"Damn it, Heather, I could make it so good!"

"Not tonight."

He hesitated, hunting furiously through his mind for arguments that might work, sensual logic that would make her rethink her decision. But there was nothing he could use short of sheer physical force, and that was not an option.

Accepting the inevitable, Jake pulled back, lifting himself to a sitting position. The half-filled glass of cognac caught his brooding eye and he reached for it, taking a healthy swallow while Heather quickly adjusted her clothing. Grimly he let the fire of fine brandy fight the fire of unsatisfied desire, curious in an almost detached way to see which element would win the battle.

"I'd better be on my way." Heather finished adjusting her dress and got to her feet. The sweep of her sleek, bluntly cut hair swung forward to shield her expression for a few critical seconds. By the time the bronzed locks were back round her ears, her face was composed and calm. Only the remnants of passion flared now in her steady gaze.

"I'll walk you back to your cottage."

"That's not necessary. The security guards will be making their rounds and heaven knows we don't get much crime out here," she reminded him with a determined breeziness. She ran her fingers lightly through her hair and started for the door. "I'll see you for breakfast in the morning, Jake. Mom and Dad will want to rehash the party and I'm sure they'll want you to join us."

"I'll walk you back to your place, Heather." Jake got to his feet, reaching the door ahead of her and taking her wrist tightly between the fingers of his right hand.

If she could recover so quickly; so could he. Even if it almost killed him! "I wouldn't want you to think I'm not a *complete* gentleman."

"The thought never crossed my mind," she assured him too blandly.

He walked her down the path through the gardens in silence and left her at her door just as she wished. He stood quietly in the shadows as she smiled good-night and stepped inside. Instead of leaving he waited a few seconds longer until he heard the click of the bolt being locked into place.

Was she double-locking the door on general principles or against him specifically?

One more week.

As he turned away it occurred to Jake that a part of him hoped she had slid that bolt in place out of some primitive caution toward him. He wanted her to think about him tonight; to remember the passion that had sparked between them. He didn't want her climbing into bed and drifting off to sleep on a cloud of anticipation about taking over the running of Hacienda Strand.

If she had locked her door against him it might mean she would not be able to get him out of her mind tonight.

In another week he would be her husband and in a position to make certain he was the last thing on her mind every night.

4

"YOU KNOW YOU WERE absolutely right about that dress last night," Ruth Strand told her daughter approvingly the next morning on the terrace as they waited for Paul and Jake to join them for breakfast. "I had my doubts at first but it struck just the right note. It was sophisticated and eye-catching and you wore it with perfect self-confidence. The only one I know who apparently objected was Jake."

"Jake? He didn't say anything about it." Heather tilted a curious eyebrow. The memory of how he'd had that beautiful silk dress crumpled around her waist flashed through her head yet again. His lovemaking had been the last thing on her mind before she'd gone to sleep, and the lush unnerving image of herself, half-naked and responding to Jake's touch, had kept her awake for a long while. A part of her had been stunned to discover that she was capable of such aching passion. It was deeply disturbing this morning to remember how close to surrender she had been last night. She wondered uneasily if Jake had been aware of the fragile control she'd had on herself.

Ruth was chuckling as she poured coffee. "I understand from Paul that he made some comment about having you give it to the Salvation Army."

"Fortunately Jake had enough sense not to make the same remark to me," Heather said dryly. Grimly she pushed the disquieting memories of the previous evening out of her head. She was back in charge of herself this morning.

"I'm not surprised he kept his mouth shut. I think he's still a little wary of you, dear. Just as you are of him. The two of you tread very carefully around each other, don't you?"

"In some ways. We're still getting to know each other, Mom."

Ruth leaned forward. "If you'd rather wait a few more weeks before you get married, it can be arranged. I must admit, as much as Paul and I wanted this marriage we were both a little surprised when you set the date so quickly."

"Tell everyone on that huge guest list that the wedding's been postponed?" Heather gasped in mock shock. "I couldn't bear that kind of responsibility." She gave her mother a quick grin. "Don't worry. I know what I'm doing. Jake and I have discussed the matter in-depth. I want the wedding over and done while things are relatively slow around the Hacienda. There just won't be time to arrange everything once the season gets into full swing."

Ruth looked at her searchingly. "But when it comes right down to it, you really haven't known each other very long, have you? I mean, you've met him a few times during the past couple of years when you came to Tucson for holiday visits, but that's about it."

"You and Dad both seemed quite certain it would be a perfect match," Heather reminded her mother calmly. "Don't tell me you're having doubts?"

"Well, no, it's just that marriage is such a big step and I want you to be sure, darling."

Heather took pity on her worried mother. Smiling reassuringly she reached out to pat her hand. "It's all right, Mom. I know what I'm doing."

"You've had that rather frightening self-assurance ever since you went away to California all those years ago," Ruth sighed. "Other than letting us know you were all right, you wouldn't even tell us what you were doing until you'd enrolled yourself in college and had a job. That first year when you agreed to come home for Christmas we didn't know what to expect. But the moment you walked in the door I knew you had grown up overnight. It was scary in a way. And every year after that you seemed to grow stronger and more certain of yourself."

"I didn't give myself much choice."

"No. Perhaps that's what worried me."

Heather shook her head ruefully, able to make light of what had, until now, been the single most traumatic occasion in her life. "After making such a gigantic error in judgment as running off with someone like Rick Monroe, I only had two choices. One was to come crawling home on my knees."

"And the other was to tough it out, pick up the pieces and make your decision work," Ruth concluded with a depth of understanding that shook Heather. "That's exactly what your father would have done if he'd found himself in an untenable situation. That's the way he reacted when he bought this land. It was out in the middle of nowhere in those days. No one thought a resort of this size and quality could successfully survive. But every time someone told Paul he was making a mistake he became that much more determined to make it work. And it did."

"So will this marriage. After all, how can I go wrong? You and Dad both approve, it makes perfect business sense, and the groom is willing."

Ruth eyed her daughter. "About the groom...."

"He's not willing?" Heather smiled.

"Oh, he's willing. But there's something you should realize, Heather. He's a lot like you in some ways. And while I freely admit I think he'll make you an excellent husband, there are times when I worry that you don't truly understand exactly what you're getting into. You know how you and your father used to fight so fiercely. Similar temperaments can have that effect on each other."

Heather once again smiled her reassurance. "Jake and I understand each other very well on that score. The only thing we could possibly have to argue about is the Hacienda and since I'm, in the last analysis, the boss, that should limit the quarreling, don't you think?"

Ruth looked skeptical but she changed the subject at once. "Santa Fe will make a lovely spot for a honeymoon. Whose idea was that?"

Heather shrugged. "Jake's I think. I wasn't really planning on taking one."

"Well, at least you'll be having a more luxurious one than your father and I were able to afford," Ruth said chuckling. "We couldn't afford to go any farther than that old cabin Paul had for hunting up in the hills."

"I haven't thought of that place in years. It was rather fun to go up there once in a while. Has Dad used it at all lately?"

"Not since he gave up hunting in favor of golf. He claimed golf was much more of a gentleman hotelier's sport than hunting, but I think he just got tired of making a sport out of killing deer. We haven't had occasion to go up to the cabin in years. Liz and Ann and their husbands take the children up there once in a while for an outing in the mountains. That's about it."

Before Heather could continue the discussion, a cheerful greeting announced the arrival of her father. She glanced up to see him striding toward her. Jake was at his side. Paul Strand was dressed in brightly colored golfing slacks and a knit shirt in preparation for the round he intended to play later that morning. Beside him Jake looked dark and restrained. His teak-brown hair was still damp from the shower. Dressed in a pair of khaki slacks and a conservatively styled dark brown shirt, he appeared a little remote and not nearly as affable as her father.

And when her eyes met his cool gray ones, Heather realized she was learning to read that formerly unreadable gaze. There was no doubt, for example, that when he looked at her now he was remembering last night, and she sensed that he was silently challenging her to recall it. Uncomfortably Heather reached for the coffeepot, unwilling to betray the fact that last night had been on her mind all morning long. He had no need to remind her of it, she thought. No woman could possibly forget coming so close to giving herself to a man. The knowledge burned inside like a steady flame that could not be snuffed out.

"Good morning, Heather." Jake came forward and bent to brush her mouth lightly in a way that was becoming his familiar morning greeting.

"Your coffee," she offered quickly, and then chided herself for being even slightly nervous around him. Good Lord. She wasn't a teenager. She ought to have a bit more poise under the circumstances!

"Heather and I were just discussing the old cabin, dear," Ruth said as her husband sat down beside her. "I was telling her that you and I spent our honeymoon there."

Paul Strand laughed. "Did you tell her where we'll be spending our second one?"

"No, not yet. I was saving it for a wedding present."

"What's this all about?" Heather demanded, aware of Jake's hard thigh casually touching hers under the table.

"Ruth and I are going to do you both a favor and take a three-month cruise while the two of you are settling down to married life and the business of running the Hacienda." He gave his wife an affectionate smile. "Ruth's been very patient all these years. Now that we're both going to have a lot more free time we'll be doing a great deal of traveling. You and Jake won't have to worry about having us hanging around the Hacienda all year long."

"Don't let Paul make you think he's doing you any favors," Ruth said laughing. "He's set a goal of playing all the major golf courses of the world. And he can't wait to get started. Since I adore cruises we've agreed to compromise and cruise to the various islands and resorts where he wants to play golf."

"And in between cruises I will plan on playing the new Hacienda Strand course, hmm?" Paul reached for the jam pot.

"If we can get Cecil Winthrop to sell us that land," Jake agreed, his eyes on Heather. "But after the way Heather had him charmed last night I expect we can get just about anything we want from the man."

"We'll see," Heather said dismissingly. "I'm not at all sure the Hacienda needs a course of its own. And no matter how 'charmed' Cecil might be, he's not going to let that land go cheap."

"If we don't pick it up fairly quickly he'll probably sell it to someone else," Jake said carefully. "There's a corporation back east that has its eye on it. The last thing we want is a commercial establishment going up nearby. It would hurt the resort atmosphere of the Hacienda."

"We'll discuss it some other time," Heather said with polite firmness.

A sudden tense silence descended over the small table, and then Paul Strand valiantly stepped in to change the subject.

"More thunderstorms predicted for this afternoon, I hear."

What would people do without the weather as a safe topic of conversation, Heather wondered in amusement.

ON THE EVE OF HER WEDDING Heather stood quietly in the shadows of her parents' garden and watched the crowd that jammed the terrace and spilled over into the lush gardens. This last party her mother had insisted on giving was for the staff of the Hacienda. Everyone from Julian Richards to the most recently hired maid was having a ball.

Somewhere in that crowd Jake was probably standing alone, sipping a glass of Scotch on the rocks while the cheerful hotel workers ebbed and flowed around him. Heather wondered if anyone had missed her yet.

Normally she would have been in the middle of the crowd, pouring her energy into playing the perfect hostess. But about an hour ago she had suddenly realized that she needed a breather. For some reason she had begun to feel a little trapped, hemmed in by people and the sure unalterable course she had set for herself.

She was going to be married in the morning. That reality had finally struck her. She intended to link her life to her career with those of a man she didn't truly know or completely comprehend.

Bridal jitters, she reassured herself. Or too much champagne. One of the two. With a wry expression she glanced down at the empty glass in her hand and wondered what Jake was thinking as the crowd milled around him.

Ever since the night of that other party, he had kept his lovemaking restrained to a few good-night kisses. There had been no more attempts to talk her into bed. Perhaps he was saving the arguments for the wedding night. Or perhaps he really intended to let her set the pace of their growing intimacy.

Controlling that pace was something Heather fully intended to do. She was, oddly enough, getting more nervous about that aspect of the marriage than she had expected. There was no denying the attraction that flared between herself and the man she was marrying. But she sensed an implicit menace in the idea of succumbing to that attraction. It was a menace she couldn't understand or explain, but it was there.

Bridal jitters, indeed!

The real problem, Heather decided abruptly, was that she was getting restless. Her family and Jake had more or less forced her to concentrate her full efforts on the wedding. In a misguided attempt to give her a small "vacation" before she assumed the reins of the Hacienda, they had all conspired to keep her away from the business offices. In an effort to oblige everyone, she had allowed herself to give complete attention to the coming wedding.

As a result she had not had anything else to take her mind off the matter. Some real work would have given her some balance during the past few weeks. She liked work. She needed it at times. Work had given her so much during the past few years. And running the Hacienda Strand was going to be so much richer and more fulfilling than anything else she had done to date.

Her family and Jake just hadn't understood that by keeping her away from the hotel offices they hadn't made things easier for her. Heather glanced around at the moonlit garden and smiled to herself. Soon everything would be settled and back under control.

"And soon, as the saying goes, all this will be mine," she joked softly to herself. When she was back at work she would feel back to normal.

Maybe what she needed to counteract the bridal jitters was some of that very therapy. On a sudden impulse Heather started down a deserted path toward the main lodge.

The fine, pleated, full-length evening gown she was wearing drifted sensually around her ankles as she made her way in silence. No one called after her or demanded to know where she was going. For the moment she was free.

The freedom, Heather discovered as she slipped into the main lodge and down the hall to the darkened offices, felt surprisingly good. For a month she had been playing the perfect daughter and the perfect fiancée. Conscious of her coming responsibilities as owner of the Hacienda Strand she had also been careful to play the gracious boss in front of the staff. The roles were all satisfying to some degree and she knew inside herself where to draw the necessary lines. No one would take advantage of her.

But occasionally a woman needed to be by herself. Tonight was one of those occasions.

The office door was locked. Going back to the front desk where only one clerk was on duty she flashed her most winning smile and asked for the key.

"Thank you, Harry. Did you enjoy the party earlier this evening?"

"Oh, yes, Miss Strand." The young desk clerk beamed. "Had a great time. Almost forgot to come back and relieve David so that he could go! Is it over?"

"No, I just decided to take a little break. This staff certainly knows how to party! I don't think anyone's even going to miss me for a while." Heather closed her fingers around the key and nodded as she went back down the hall.

A few moments later she stepped inside the plush offices that belonged to her father until tomorrow morning. This would be her domain, Heather thought wonderingly as she trailed a finger along the mahogany desk top. Moving slowly, she walked across the thick rug to the wall of files. Soon she would be in charge of her beloved Hacienda.

All those years in California away from the place she loved so much. It seemed like a lifetime. But now she was home.

The deep leather chair behind the desk looked inviting. With a smile of distinct pleasure Heather sank down in it. How many times had she wandered into this office as a child and clambered over this chair? So many memories. And not all of them bad. It was only in her teen years that the temperaments of her father and herself had truly begun to clash. During those unstable years when she had been growing from child into woman, things had been tense and difficult. She had never stopped loving her father or the rest of her family. But she had needed to separate herself from the domineering influences in her life. Needed to prove herself and make her own way.

And that was exactly what she'd succeeded in doing. She had needed those years in California and the task of proving herself to herself and her family had been accomplished. It was time to come home.

Absently she began opening desk drawers. With a pleasant sensation of possessiveness she regarded the array of pens and pencils and paper clips in the center drawer and then shut it. The drawers on the left side yielded a battered dictionary and stationery with the Hacienda Strand letterhead. The Tucson phone book was stashed in the back.

The right-hand drawers were locked. Experimentally Heather tugged at them, trying to remember where her father had always kept the key. Ah, yes. Behind the row of books on the top shelf of the bookcase across the room.

On a whim Heather got up and went over to the case. Standing on tiptoe she scrabbled around behind a copy of a history of Arizona until her fingertips closed over the little key. Then she went back to the desk and unlocked the drawers.

This was where her father had always kept the most vital financial records. The corporation's check registers, bank-account information, various licenses were all still neatly filed here.

Strange. Jake had taken over much of the day-to-day accounting work during the past two years. Heather wondered why a great deal of the financial information hadn't been transferred to his office. From what she had been able to tell, Jake appeared to work out of his cottage.

With idle curiosity she pulled one of the journals out of the drawer and began flipping through it. Perhaps her father hadn't been very good at delegating authority. When she took over next week she would see to it that Jake took charge of these records. After all, he was supposed to be the financial wizard. He should have custody of the journals and ledgers and other such records.

Her eye paused on some recent entries, noting that the handwriting was not her father's or that of his secretary. It was strong masculine handwriting. Jake's?

A bit more intently she began to examine the various items. She was wrong about one thing. Her father certainly had delegated authority to Jake!

Frowning intently, she reached for some of the official records of the corporation. Exactly what title did Jake hold?

Five minutes later she sat staring at the copy of a recent corporate resolution that had been drawn up to open a new checking account at a local bank. The document clearly stated the owner of the Hacienda Strand, and it was not Paul Strand.

Stunned, Heather read the name again and again, unable to comprehend what she was seeing in black and white.

Fifteen minutes later, after poring over every vital document she could find, Heather was forced to acknowledge the truth. Jake Cavender owned the Hacienda Strand, and had owned it for the past six months.

It had been about four months ago that her father had first approached her about returning to Tucson to take over the Hacienda. Three or four months ago that her parents had first begun to hint very seriously just how beneficial a marriage between herself and Jake would be for all concerned. Oh, the matchmaking had begun almost two years ago. Whenever she happened to return to Tucson for the holidays her mother had always tried to pair her with Jake. But it had been only recently that the suggestions of marriage had become so definite.

A perfect team, her father had said. A perfect management team.

No one had bothered to tell her that she was not going to be the ranking member of that team. No one had spelled out that her birthright had been sold to the man she was to marry.

Fury, intense and passionate beyond anything she had ever known, began to uncoil in her. For long moments she sat very still in the huge leather chair, not trusting her coordination. Then, very slowly she got shakily to her feet.

She had been manipulated. Cheated of her inheritance. Lured home by false promises. It had all been an elaborate illusion spun by masters. And she had fallen neatly into the trap Jake and her father had woven.

She could not believe her mother knew of the change of ownership. Her gentle mother could never have maintained such a lie. No, this was the work of hard tough businessmen. Men like Jake and Paul.

The overwhelming sense of betrayal made her momentarily dizzy. She clutched at the desk to steady herself. What a fool she had been!

No wonder Jake hadn't seriously objected to signing the prenuptial agreement. He had changed the only clause that might conceivably cause him some frustration. Everything else he had agreed to had merely been protecting his own financial interests! He was the one who was entering the marriage with control of the Ha-

cienda, and he was the one who would retain possession of it in the event the marriage was dissolved.

Calling herself a fool and an idiot in a hundred different ways, Heather managed to let herself out of the
office. She returned the key to the puzzled desk clerk
who wondered why he wasn't getting the customary
brilliant smile he had come to expect from Heather.
Then she made her way out into the comforting darkness of the gardens.

The music on her parents' terrace drifted through the
balmy night air along with the distant hubbub of the
crowd. Jake would be standing there, a remote island
in the stream, knowing he owned all he surveyed. And
tomorrow morning at ten he was scheduled to acquire
the last item on his shopping list. At ten he would have
secured not only the physical property of the Hacienda
but the intangible sensation of really belonging to it. He
would be marrying the daughter of the man who had
created the Hacienda Strand out of the desert. He would
be joining the family.

Rage and a violent sense of betrayal battled with an
even stronger feeling of utter stupidity within Heather.
How could she have been so incredibly blind? All that
talk about not letting her get into the business end of
the Hacienda until after the wedding. What a fool she
had been.

She had allowed herself to be manipulated and used;
controlled and driven in the direction Jake had determined. It might have been interesting to see how and
when he would finally have broken the truth to her,
Heather thought in chilled fury.

"Hello, Heather. I've been looking for you."

Her head snapped around. Jake was standing nearby, his face in deep shadow. It was as if her enraged imagination had conjured him up out of the darkness. A devil who had come to buy her soul. And she had almost sold it. More than almost, Heather was forced to acknowledge. By owning the Hacienda, he already owned a large chunk of it.

"Good evening, Jake. Have you been enjoying yourself?" From out of nowhere an icy calm settled on her.

"Not particularly. But everyone else seems to be having a good time." He was still standing in darkness. She could barely see the narrowed gleam of his eyes, let alone read those unfathomable gray depths.

"You'll have to start learning how to have a good time too, won't you? After all, you're making the resort life a career, aren't you?"

His face hardened as she began to step past him, and he reached out to catch her wrist. "Heather? Are you all right?"

Frantically she summoned a bright smile. "Of course. Why shouldn't I be?"

"You've never left one of these parties early. You always seem to enjoy playing hostess."

"I needed a little time to myself." She let her glance slide away from his implacably concerned expression.

"Bridal jitters?" he offered.

"Umm, yes. I expect so."

"That's not like you, either, is it?"

"Jake, as I keep pointing out to you, you don't really know me that well, do you?" she sighed.

"I'm learning."

It sounded like a threat. Heather reacted by carefully freeing her wrist and stepping away from him. She kept the too-bright smile in place. "If you don't mind, I'd better be getting back to the party. My mother will be wondering where I am."

"I'll come with you."

She could say nothing in opposition. But when he again caught her hand in his she shivered and knew he felt it.

"Heather?"

"Bridal jitters, as you said, Jake. Don't worry, I'll be fine by tomorrow. Back to normal, in fact."

"Good. Because it's much too late to change your plans." When she shot him a wary sidelong glance he gave her an amused look. "Two hundred people in the resort chapel and no telling how many at the reception. Julian would have a fit if he had to throw all those hors d'oeuvres away."

"Don't worry, Jake, I'll show up at the wedding. After all, it's my first one and I'm bound to be curious." She slipped free of his grasp once more as the good-natured crowd on the terrace closed around them.

Heather spotted Jim Connors, the busboy who owned the beautiful new motorcycle, and moved to join the group with whom he was standing. As usual he was discussing the intricacies of motorcycle riding with his friends, and Heather, aware that she was a few years out-of-date, joined right in.

When the party was over the problem of how to avoid finding herself alone with Jake was readily solved when she found herself amid a group of hotel workers who were going in her general direction. At her door she bid them all good-night, including Jake who stood on the fringes, watching her through cool considering eyes. With another overly brilliant smile she closed the door on everyone.

AT NINE-FIFTEEN the next morning Heather dismissed her mother and her sisters with a firmness that surprised everyone, including herself. For the past hour they had been fluttering around the bride-to-be, arranging the elegant lace-and-satin gown, experimenting with her hair under the gossamer veil, telling her how lovely she looked. Their excitement should have been contagious but Heather had been growing increasingly high-strung and chilled. With forty-five minutes to go before she was due at the quiet chapel tucked into the hotel gardens, Heather could take the warmth and family affection no longer. The falseness of the entire situation had to be ended.

"I just need a little time to myself," she explained, waving them all out the front door. "Don't worry, I'm quite capable of walking over to the chapel on my own."

"Heather, dear, are you feeling all right?" Ruth Strand asked anxiously.

"I'm fine, Mother. Just a little tense."

Her mother smiled. "Perhaps a bit of sherry before the wedding?"

Ann, Heather's youngest sister, looked horrified. "Mother! That's outrageous!"

"Actually, it sounds like a rather good idea, but I think I'll pass," Heather said wryly.

"All right, dear. Call if you need us," Ruth said, her blue eyes reflecting her feminine understanding of the strain her daughter was experiencing.

Except that her mother couldn't possibly know just how bad the strain was, Heather told herself wearily as she shut the door behind the female members of her family. No one could possibly understand.

It seemed to take forever to undo the row of buttons that ran down the back of the elegant summer wedding gown. Heather worked with a grim intensity that grew as the dress crumpled into a frothy heap around her feet. Then she unfastened the pale stockings and rolled them down to her toes. When she lifted the veil she was left standing in the silky white bra and panties. For a long moment Heather studied her reflection in the mirror seeking guidance or answers or assurance that could never come.

Then she turned to her closet and pulled out the narrow black designer jeans she had bought for horseback riding. When they were fastened she tugged a black cotton-knit pullover out of her drawer and located the sleek leather riding boots standing in the back of the closet. She controlled the sweep of bronzed hair with a headband she had bought to wear for tennis. It had a vague Southwest-Indian motif woven into it and it went rather strikingly with the silver-and-leather belt she wrapped around her narrow waist.

This time when she glanced into the mirror there was no trace of a glowing bride. A proud, coldly angry woman stared back at her. A woman who looked as though she could take care of herself in a man's world.

It was exactly the image Heather needed to see in that moment. Deliberately she turned away and headed for the door.

She found Jim Connors hanging around the back of the hotel kitchens, enjoying a soft drink with some of his friends as he took a break before the lunch rush. When she offered him fifty dollars for temporary use of his new motorcycle he stared at her.

"Don't worry, Jim. I know what I'm doing on a bike. And the fifty will go a long way toward gas." She smiled at him with a cool imperiousness that made him obey. Uncertainly he dug the keys out of his jeans.

"Uh, the wedding?" he asked hesitantly, clearly out of his depths.

"The wedding is on schedule as far as I know." She plucked the keys from his hesitant grasp and replaced them with fifty dollars in cash. "Thanks. I'll make sure you get it back in one piece."

"Miss Strand, I don't know about this," the teenager said worriedly.

"Oh, one more thing. Would you mind if I borrowed your leather jacket? For safety purposes."

"Well, no, I guess not. It will be a little big. Look, Miss Strand, maybe you should borrow the bike another time?"

"Now is exactly the right time." She shrugged into the leather jacket. The desert sun would rapidly make the garment uncomfortable but she could live with that.

The massive black motorcycle accepted her unprotestingly. She mounted automatically from the left side, her jeaned leg swinging expertly over the seat, and the helmet stowed behind. The twisting grip that was the accelerator fit perfectly in her right hand. It had been a long time but when she experimentally took the powerful bike around the employee parking lot everything came back, including the incomparable rush of excitement and independence. The feelings were a drug in her veins. Without further hesitation Heather headed the bike for the exit. She didn't glance back at Jim's anxious face.

The narrow path that wound picturesquely up to the little chapel was almost empty. Most of the guests were already seated or standing around in the gardens, chatting as they waited for the services to begin. Bright flutters of colorful dresses were scattered like flowers. The men's clothing was not quite as bright but it certainly reflected the sunbelt dress code. Everyone looked cheerful and light and pleasantly excited.

The politely threatening but subdued roar of the black cycle made everyone turn toward Heather as she rode the bike slowly up the path. For a moment no one recognized her, including her parents and Jake who were standing together on the front steps of the chapel.

Jake realized first who it was. He didn't move as she drove the big bike to the bottom of the steps and halted it. One booted foot bracing herself and the machine, Heather flexed her fingers on the handlebars and focused only on the man who waited for her. She refused to look at the mingled shock and anxiety on her mother's face or the stunned outrage on her father's.

Jake watched her as though she were a sorceress who was about to cast an evil spell on him. His hard face revealed nothing of what he was thinking. He stood impassive and remote as he awaited the bolt of lightning she was about to throw. Of all the people gathered there only he seemed to realize exactly what was happening.

"I understand there's a wedding here today," Heather remarked so that all could hear. "I just wanted to come by and congratulate the groom. I understand he's the new owner of the Hacienda Strand. The news came as something of a shock to the bride, I'm afraid, so if I were you I wouldn't stand around waiting for her. She's a bit indisposed at the moment. Feeling like a manipulated idiot will do that to a woman. Especially on her wedding day.

"But don't let that little fact ruin the celebration. I'm sure the groom is quite capable of carrying on without her. After all, he's got everything else, including the bride's inheritance. I know he can make do without the bride herself. As for the bride, well, she'll be okay, too. She's had a lot of experience taking care of herself and she intends to apply it. You all have a good time now, you hear?"

She twisted the accelerator in her right hand and the bike growled in response. The fluttery dresses and handsome suits standing in the way parted instantly, creating a path for the black beast Heather rode. She roared down the path toward the main entrance to the lodge and then she was free, heading down the road toward Tucson.

Behind her, stunned silence hung thickly in the air as the assembled guests turned to stare at the groom where he stood with the bride's parents.

Jake watched impassively as Heather disappeared into the distance, and then he spoke calmly to the man who had just missed becoming his father-in-law.

"Didn't you ever tell Heather to wear a helmet when she went motorcycle riding?"

Paul Strand nearly chocked on his answer. "More often than I can remember."

"Well, this time I'll have to see that she gets the message." Jake strode down the steps and the crowd at the bottom parted for him in the same way they had parted for the woman on the motorcycle.

Perhaps they sensed a similar potential for raw violence in man and machine.

5

THE RIDE INTO TUCSON provided everything Heather needed at that moment. The instant responses of the motorcycle, so much faster and more accurate than an automobile, required her full attention. The sensation of speed fed her need for physical excitement. And the adrenaline pounding through her blood consumed the element of danger that flowed through the air around her. She was at one with the big machine, and for the length of time it took to reach the main part of town, Heather knew a violent sense of satisfaction.

The satisfaction began to fade when she was forced to slow for the first stoplight. Reality slowly settled, extending its long coils to imprison her.

Heather realized she had no clear-cut idea of what she intended to do next. The logical step was to hop the next flight back to California. She could hardly take Jim Connors's beautiful motorcycle all the way to San Francisco.

At least this time she would be leaving town with more than a few dollars to her name, Heather thought wryly as she pulled into a gas station and halted the bike beside a phone booth. Tucked away in the small built-in carrier of the motorcycle was her checkbook and stuffed into her calfskin wallet were several credit cards. She wouldn't have to find work in a fast-food restaurant in order to survive. The checking account and the credit cards were all her own. There was not a dime of her father's money involved.

"Hey, lady, quite a bike. Want to give me a ride?" The grinning face of the gas-station attendant caught Heather's attention.

"Not today."

Stuffing the keys into her front pocket Heather stepped into the phone booth and started calling airlines. The next flight to San Francisco wasn't until later that evening. Yes, there was one seat left. Heather took it.

The gas-station attendant and some of his buddies were hovering around the bike when she emerged.

"Kind of a big bike for a little lady like you," one volunteered with an experimental leer.

"I manage." She tossed her hair back and boldly stepped toward the bike, daring any of the curious young men to get in her way.

They moved aside, just as the wedding guests had done. Everyone, it seemed, knew better than to get in her way today, Heather reflected bitterly.

She had several hours to kill before leaving for the airport. It was getting far too hot to spend them outside. The thought of killing time in one of the huge indoor shopping malls appealed briefly before she discarded it. The last thing she wanted was to be surrounded by people. She needed some time to think. Everything had happened so fast since her discovery last night.

Someplace cool and quiet. A motel room.

Slowly Heather began to cruise toward the airport, seeking one of the new motels that had been built near it. Some time later a frankly suspicious desk clerk handed her the key to Room 235.

"Complimentary coffee and rolls in the morning," he volunteered.

"Fine." She saw no reason to inform him she'd be gone by then.

In the anonymous room on the second floor she sat down on the bed and picked up the telephone. Jim Connors was going to be frantic about his beloved bike. Refusing to identify herself, she waited impatiently until the young busboy could be found and brought to the front-desk phone.

"Jim? It's Heather."

"Geez! Am I glad to hear from you. Is the bike okay?"

"Of course. I'm calling to tell you where you can pick it up. Sorry I'm not going to be able to return it myself, but I trust the fifty I gave you will pay for the inconvenience."

"Miss Strand, everything's in a mess here. Chef Richards is causing the biggest scene in the kitchen and everyone's saying you split."

"Everyone's right. Jim, listen to me. It's very important to me that no one knows where I am just now. Do you understand?"

"But what about my bike?"

"I'm going to leave your bike in the parking lot of a motel. The keys will be at the front desk."

"What motel?" he begged, clearly beginning to panic.

"One out by the airport. I'll call you later and tell you exactly which one, okay?"

"But, Miss Strand . . . !"

"I'll leave another fifty in an envelope along with the keys. Goodbye Jim, and thanks." Heather replaced the phone before the teenager could argue.

Then she threw herself back against the pillows, one booted leg drawn up heedlessly on the flower-patterned bedspread. *God in heaven, what a mess.*

She didn't even have the excuse of being eighteen this time. Heather covered her eyes with her arm and tried to think. All these years of taking care of herself, of growing and achieving and building a career. She had thrown all that away for the elusive promise of coming home.

She ought to have known it just wasn't going to be that easy.

The hours stretched out ahead of her. Hours in which to think about the disaster. The image of her mother's appalled hurt gaze haunted her. This was the second time Heather had been responsible for putting that look in her mother's eyes. Jim Connors's fears for his precious bike elicited another wave of guilt. She'd used the poor boy, no doubt about it. And then there was her father, humiliated in front of all his friends. She knew in her heart of hearts Paul Strand had honestly convinced himself he was doing what was best for Heather by manipulating her into marriage with the new owner of the Hacienda Strand. Heather realized that her father had never actually lied to her. He had never told her she was inheriting the Hacienda. But there were such things as lies by omission and implication.

Nothing at all could excuse Jake Cavender. He had known exactly what he was doing and there had been no other motivation except sheer self-interest. He'd wanted to secure his position at the Hacienda and in the Strand family.

Depression welled up to take over the unnatural, somewhat savage high Heather had found herself riding. And with the depression came the hot stinging tears. Heather gave in to them, seeking the odd relief they offered. And when the scalding flow finally ceased, she lay staring at the ceiling, unable to slip into the temporary oblivion of sleep.

How long she lay that way, haunted by memories and guilt and seething anger, Heather didn't know. Outside the afternoon thunderstorm formed, dropped their torrents of rain and slowly dissipated. In another couple of hours she would be able to call a cab to the airport.

There was no knock on her door. It simply swung open without any warning as a key was slipped into the outside lock. Heather's startled eyes went to the doorway, even as some feminine instinct warned her who would be standing there.

"Jake."

"We almost got through it without any hitches, didn't we? I should have realized things were going a little too smoothly." He pocketed the motel-room key.

Some part of Heather's disoriented brain insisted on noting that he was dressed in a manner quite different from his normal attire. Instead of the well-tailored slacks he usually wore, Jake had on a pair of jeans. A khaki shirt, worn leather belt and a pair of desert boots completed the outfit.

"What are you doing here?" Heather whispered. "How did you find me?"

"I found you after the Connors kid began to panic over the fate of his bike. He told me he'd heard from you and that you said you'd be leaving the bike in one of the motel parking lots near the airport. That really pinned it down geographically. A few phone calls and I got lucky. The desk clerk thought you looked a bit suspicious. He didn't hesitate at all when I asked him for the key to your room."

"I see. I wasn't thinking too clearly, I guess," she said bitterly, sitting up slowly on the bed. "But then I haven't really been thinking clearly for the past month or I would have realized what a fool I was. You didn't answer my first question, Jake. What are you doing here? If you've come to drag your errant bride home, you're wasting your time."

"Am I?" He closed the door behind him with a final-sounding click.

Heather stood up, feeling too vulnerable in a sitting position. Standing didn't help a great deal, she discovered. She still felt too vulnerable. There was something far too intimidating about Jake Cavender this evening. It was as if the careful remote mask he had always worn in her presence had disintegrated. The controlled savagery that had replaced it was far from reassuring.

"Be satisfied with what you've got, Jake," she mocked harshly. "Take it from me, you don't get everything you want in life."

"Perhaps not, but I can take a damn good shot at it." He took a step toward her and halted.

"You don't need me. You've got the Hacienda and you've got the goodwill and affection of my family. Believe me, after today they'll probably cast me out of the family altogether and put you in my place. As long as you're here, though, would you mind answering a few questions?"

"Why not? I'm willing to talk before proceeding to the next step."

"Bastard," she breathed tightly.

"Is that a question or a comment? Whichever it is, it happens to be true in a technical sense." Jake sank fluidly in the room's only chair, stretching out his long jeaned legs. His gray eyes never wavered. "I didn't have the advantage of growing up in a home where I really belonged, Heather. For me it was one foster home after another after my mother finally gave up trying to support me and a drinking habit, too. My father wasn't in the picture long enough to worry about supporting anything or anyone."

"I'm not in the mood for a sob story, Jake."

"Because it makes you feel guilty? You can handle that, Heather. You've had to deal with guilt more than once in your life, haven't you? To tell you the truth, though, I wasn't trying to make you feel guilty or even a little sorry for me. I was trying to explain why I'm capable of appreciating what you so blithely are willing to toss aside whenever things aren't going exactly as you'd like them to go."

"I have nothing left to blithely toss aside. You bought it, lock, stock and barrel six months ago!"

He eyed her thoughtfully for a long moment. "You found out last night, didn't you? During that period when you disappeared from the staff party. What were you doing, Heather? Ransacking the office?"

"I was under the illusion that the office was mine. I thought I was merely going through my own files," she raged.

"The office and the files belong to us. You and me."

"The hell they do," she muttered seethingly. "You own the Hacienda. And any right I might have had to the place as your wife I signed away myself when I had that prenuptial agreement drawn up. How you must have laughed that night when you agreed to sign! My God, Jake. Just because I've been a complete fool for the past month, give me some credit for basic intelligence."

"Your father fully intended for both of us to be running the Hacienda Strand when he sold out to me," Jake told her levelly.

"Oh, yes, I remember. The famous management team we're supposed to make. It may sound lovely in theory but we both know there can never be two people sharing equally in that kind of control. In the final analysis there can only be one boss. And guess who that one boss will be?"

"We're going to be a team, Heather."

"Uh huh. You want an example of teamwork in action? Suppose I decided I definitely don't want to put in that golf course. What will you do then?" she challenged, beginning to pace restlessly in the confined space available.

There was silence from Jake's chair. When she swung around to confront him he was watching her broodingly.

"Well?" she prodded.

"I want the golf course built."

"And in the end, because you own the place, you'll go ahead and build it. Regardless of my decision. There wouldn't be one single thing I could do to stop you. That's the way the tough decisions would always go. You own Hacienda Strand and, in the final analysis, you'll make the major choices for the hotel's future. I'm nothing if not realistic when it comes to business, Jake, so don't try to con me." She wrapped her arms across her breasts, tensely rubbing her arms. "Heaven knows I've been conned enough recently."

"I asked you more than once if running the Hacienda was all you came back here for. You told me there was a lot more to it than that. You said you wanted a home, roots, a sense of belonging. You said you wanted to be a part of the heritage of your father's hotel. You can have all that, Heather. But there's a price for everything."

"An honest businessman would have told me the full price long before now," she murmured.

"You never asked. You just assumed you knew the full picture. Did you really think you could just come back to Tucson and take over? Did you think everything had been placed in a neat little time warp for you? That things have stood still awaiting the return of the queen? I arrived here two years ago because your father wanted some expert consulting advice. The Hacienda was in trouble, Heather."

"I don't believe you!"

"Believe what you want. I'm telling you the truth. I had recently pulled a couple of major hotels out of the red and put them back on their feet. Your father needed that kind of expertise and he needed it badly. He had the sense to listen to me. But advice wasn't all he needed. The hotel needed an infusion of capital and I provided that."

"My father was in your debt?" she demanded incredulously.

"He could have repaid it once the hotel was back in smooth waters. That happened about eight months ago. But by then I knew I wanted to be a part of the place. Somehow the Hacienda had become home. I knew your father was getting tired of the responsibility of running it and that he had always hoped you would take it over. But no one knew what you were going to do. And, to tell you the truth, I personally didn't think you deserved the place."

"So you set yourself up as judge and jury. Talk about arrogance!"

"I wanted the Hacienda. And after I'd met you a couple of times, I realized that the hotel wasn't all I wanted. Marrying you would satisfy your father's longing to keep the place in the family. I wanted him to be completely happy with the deal, and I decided that marrying you would satisfy me, as well. By the time you proposed your little business bargain I was sure of it. I had told Ruth when he agreed to sell me the Hacienda six months ago that I would make every effort to marry you. We agreed to keep our arrangement quiet until we could find out whether or not you and I would mesh."

"Well, you have your answer on that issue now!"

"Yes, I think I do. We mesh very well, Heather Strand. The only glitch at the moment is your pride. Once you've had a chance to cool down I think you can be made to see that the deal between us is a good one."

"Will you stop referring to our marriage as a business arrangement?" she hissed.

"You're the one who set it up that way. Prenuptial contract and all."

"Why am I standing here arguing with you?" she asked more or less of the ceiling. "I've got a plane to catch in an hour."

"No you don't. I canceled your reservation."

"You what?"

"I called the airport before I called the motels. When I found out you had a reservation on the evening flight to San Francisco, I canceled it."

"That changes nothing. I'll stay here tonight and catch the morning flight."

"You're right about staying here tonight. We can discuss the morning flight tomorrow afternoon." He gave her his slow, quietly amused smile, but the reckless fire in his gray gaze flared as he spoke.

"If you're implying that you intend to spend the night with me, you can think again, Jake Cavender. You must be out of your mind if you really believe I'd let you stay here."

"This was supposed to be our wedding night," he reminded her silkily.

"An interesting thought. When would you have bothered to tell me about the fact that you owned the hotel? Before you seduced me? Perhaps the next morn-

ing over breakfast? What a lovely wedding gift the news
would have made."

He exhaled slowly. "Paul and I knew that if you realized your father had sold the Hacienda, you would
never come home."

"How brilliantly astute of you!"

"I also realized, and Paul agreed, that you weren't
likely to give any relationship between you and me
much of a chance if you thought I owned the Hacienda."

"So the two of you set out to manipulate me," she
concluded furiously.

"We let nature take its course. No one ever lied to
you, Heather. You just made some assumptions and
neither your father nor I corrected them. Partially because, to a large extent, they were valid. You and I are
going to run that hotel together. And I know we can
have a good marriage."

"What do you know about good marriages?" she
raged, spinning around once more to face him.

"I know that we've got the ingredients. You yourself
pointed them out. We've got some powerful business
interests in common. We've got a mutual desire to make
a home and a career out of Hacienda Strand. We both
want to please your parents and, finally, we both want
each other. That's a better basis than most couples start
out with!"

"Go to hell!"

"Can you deny any single one of those factors?" he
pushed deliberately.

"I don't have to accept or deny anything. And if we're
going to make lists, how about one that includes a

marriage based on lies and deceit. What kind of a chance would it have? What woman wants a husband who knowingly misled her?"

"I did what I had to do to make the whole arrangement work," he shot back stonily, getting to his feet.

Instinctively Heather stopped pacing and took half a step back. "Including using sex!"

"No, that's the one tactic I really didn't try. I always let you stop me. I let you have control of that aspect of the situation. But I'm beginning to think I made a serious tactical error on that point. I should have taken you to bed a couple of weeks ago, Heather Strand. I should have made you realize just how much you and I want each other."

"You think sex would have solved everything? Made matters easy for you?" she scoffed, retreating another pace as he advanced slowly. The situation was out of control and she knew it. It was out of control because she herself had slipped her own leash. The chains of controlled focused behavior she had put on herself so many years ago had started to weaken last night as she sat in the Hacienda Strand's offices and faced the truth.

The only explanation for her wildly stormy behavior that morning was that those chains had parted altogether. The passionate spirited girl had turned into a woman but the volatile element of her nature had not been destroyed. It had merely been kept buried under guard.

Heather knew what was happening in herself and it frightened her. It also left her feeling strangely exhilarated as she faced the man responsible for loosing the strong emotions within her. She hadn't allowed herself to feel such fierce emotion of any kind in so many years that the result was almost dizzying.

Jake, too, was intuitive enough to realize what had happened, and he knew he was dealing with fire. If he didn't control it the resulting blaze might consume them both, he told himself.

"You didn't handle matters very well this morning, did you, Heather? You've been sitting in this hotel room for the past few hours wishing you'd found another way to deal with the sense of betrayal you felt. You've been seeing the pain on your mother's face. The humiliation your sisters went through. The anger and hurt your father experienced. Just like last time—you couldn't come back and face the havoc you caused eleven years ago. You just kept going. But this time you know you can't run. This time you have to go back and deal with it like the adult woman you are. There's only one person you can blame for your present situation besides yourself, and that's me. I'm the one who convinced your father to keep quiet about the sale of the Hacienda. He didn't even tell your mother. I told Paul it would be the best way to handle you."

"You manipulated me as though I was a rival! A threat to your position."

"You were. I couldn't risk telling you everything until I had you committed to me, as well as to the Hacienda Strand."

"Such arrogance."

"Was I any more arrogant than you were to think you could descend on the Hacienda after all these years and pick up where you left off? I'm the one who poured money and time and everything else I had to give into that hotel during the past two years. I'm the one Paul Strand came to when the place was in trouble and I'm the one who put it back on its feet. It's going to be my home and it can be yours, as well. If you come home with me everything can fall back into place."

"You're crazy if you think I'll come back with you."

"It's the only option you've got that you can live with and you know it."

"That's not true."

"The only other option is to run off to California again. Do you really want me to let you do that?"

"I'm not a child. You're not going to decide what I do or which option I'll choose," she flashed. The feeling of entrapment grew stronger, making her desperate in a way she hadn't been in years. Like a cornered animal she scrambled for an escape. There was none.

"Heather, every argument you used with me the night you proposed still exists and is still valid. The only difference is that you now know I own the Hacienda."

"That's a rather huge difference!"

"No, it's not. Once you've accepted it, recovered from the shock of finding out you're not going to be the only one in charge, you'll see that I'm right. Everything can be exactly as we both want. We'll have our home and our combined interest in the Hacienda. You'll have achieved everything you came back to achieve. Including the happiness of your family."

He was throwing her a lifeline and Heather knew it. It would be embarrassing going back after that scene this morning but it would be a nine-day wonder that would eventually die down. Life could go back to normal in some respects. She could soothe some of the pain and humiliation she had caused her family.

Wearily Heather lowered herself to the bed, rubbing her forehead with her hand. "What have you done to me, Jake? I can't even think straight."

"Only because you've been so busy painting yourself into a corner." He stretched out a strong hand. "Come with me, honey. I can help you out of that corner."

She stared at his hand. "You're the one who got me into it in the first place."

He drew a breath. "We both made mistakes because we both wanted the Hacienda and everything it means. But there's something else we both want just as much, Heather. Each other."

"Don't play any more games with me, Jake. I've had all I can take today."

Jake moved to stand in front of her using his extended hand to stroke the curve of her head. Heather flinched but she didn't try to evade him. "It's true and you know it, don't you? The attraction between us is very, very strong. It's a wonder one of us hasn't given into it."

"Probably because we've both had our eyes on more important things," Heather snapped. "The Hacienda, for example."

"No, I don't think that's the reason. I've held back because I didn't want to risk upsetting you. I've been trying to play that side of things strictly as you ordered. Give me credit for that much, at any rate. Why have you been holding back?"

"I told you. I had other, more important things on my mind." She tried to move and found it impossible. He was standing directly in front of her as she sat on the bed. His legs were slightly apart, caging hers, and his hand was still stroking her hair.

"I don't think that was the reason at all. I think you were wary of me; perhaps even afraid because you know that when you're in bed with me you're going to lose that fine sense of poise and self-control you've worked so hard to develop. All that passion and fire and spirit are going to be set free. I won't settle for less and I think you know it."

She reacted violently to the threat in his words, surging to her feet and shoving at his lean, hard body with both hands.

"No!" The single word was torn from her lips, a cry of frustration and rage and fear.

"Heather, honey, stop it. Calm down. You can't fight me and win. Not on this level."

But she struggled to win, nevertheless, frantically trying to free herself and make for the door. In a flurry of arms and legs Jake tumbled her back onto the bed, pinning her by her wrists and using the weight of his body to hold hers quiet.

Heather stared up at him through slitted catlike eyes, her teeth slightly bared in a primitive reaction. What she read on Jake's face was not rage or disgust or violence. What she saw in the depths of those gray eyes was desperation, and the discovery of such an emotion in this man shook her to the core. It suddenly chilled her own fury and fear.

"Jake?" Dazedly she moved her head, trying to find her feet mentally if not physically. "Jake, I don't understand. What are you . . . ?"

"I can't let you go, Heather," he groaned heavily as he lowered his head. "You're a part of it. I need you to make it all work. Don't you understand?"

"No, no, I don't, and I don't want to," she heard herself say on a note of panic. The last thing she could risk was giving herself to Jake Cavender. Not now when everything had gone so terribly wrong.

"If you can walk away in the morning, after we've been together tonight, I swear I won't stop you. But I want tonight, Heather. You owe me a wedding night."

His mouth came down on hers with a rough intensity that communicated Jake's hunger all too clearly.

Frantically Heather tried to find the words she needed to free herself. She managed to pull her mouth momentarily from his. "Would you want me so much if I had nothing to do with the Hacienda? If I offered you one night instead of marriage? Would you, Jake? If you could have me only on my terms, without the security of a proper wedding and without my family's blessing, would you still think the attraction between us was so very important?"

"What the hell are you talking about?"

"Because that's all I'm willing to give a man who likes to manipulate me."

"Honey, you don't know what you're saying. You don't want a one-night stand any more than I do. You want everything right. That's why you came home. To make everything right."

Her eyes widened in anguished honesty. "I don't know what I want anymore, Jake."

She felt the tension in him. "Then we'll take it one step at a time until you do know what you want. Tonight I'll show you that one of the things you do want is me."

"If you make love to me tonight it will be on my terms," she vowed, knowing in every fiber of her being that all her defenses were down. The emotions in her were an uncontrollable flood, as violent as the seasonal thunderstorms that swept through the area on summer afternoons. Pain and passion and rebellion and rage seethed in her veins, seeking a way to release themselves. She knew instinctively that if Jake made love to her he would tap into that internal storm in her body. The prospect was both terrifying and exhilarating. "No promises, Jake. No guarantees. No neat tidy package consisting of me, my approving family and a home at the Hacienda Strand."

"Another contract, Heather? Like that prenuptial agreement you made me sign?"

"You won't sign this one because there's nothing in it for you, is there?"

"You said yourself that you don't know me very well," Jake muttered as his mouth closed once more over hers.

6

No, HEATHER REALIZED as his body shifted to crush her deeply in the bed, she didn't know him very well. If she did, she would have understood that the depths of his emotions were even more raw and powerful than her own.

She learned that shattering fact the moment he began to consume her with his passion. The spectrum of his blazing emotions was suddenly savagely revealed to her. In him there was pain and passion just as she had known. There was anger, too. And a purely masculine desire to find the key to her surrender. But above all there was a hunger unlike anything she had ever known.

There was no doubt that Jake wanted her tonight for a variety of reasons, but in that moment Heather could not believe any of them were business ones.

The caldron of emotions that were swirling in her reacted to the fundamental intensity of Jake as though they had suddenly received a focus and an outlet. All her turmoil coalesced into an unalterable sensual response that spiraled upward to meet the demands of the man who had induced the chaos.

Heather could not have said exactly what she felt as Jake sprawled across her body and plundered her mouth with his own. There was no way such fervor could be based on love, she was certain. But she had never experienced anything close to it. The urgent need to pursue the dangerous course on which she had embarked left no room for analysis.

Her nails bit deeply into the fabric of his shirt, seeking the resilient feel of his smoothly muscled shoulders. He was a strong man and discovering that his passion matched his physical strength was enthralling. She wanted to satisfy that unleashed hunger in him more than she'd ever wanted anything else in her life.

"I've been going out of my head wanting you these past few weeks," he rasped as he momentarily pulled his mouth free from hers. "I told myself I'd give you time; that I could wait until our wedding night. But when I saw you on that damn bike this morning I knew you weren't going to come tamely to my bed after all." His hand released her wrist to stroke the side of her cheek as she lay looking up at him through her lashes. "All along I've been wondering what you would be like when you weren't so busy being charming and poised. Today I'm finding out, aren't I?"

"What makes you think you're going to like me when I'm not charming and poised?"

"Liking doesn't come into it." He ran his finger along her lower lip, opening her mouth, then he leaned down again to plunge his tongue into the moist depths behind her teeth.

Heather twisted slightly beneath him, reacting to the hardening weight of his body. He responded by thrusting one of his legs between hers. As he separated her thighs he used his free hand to trail down across her breasts to the mound below her waist. His fingers

pressed against the denim of her jeans, tracing the outline of her with an intimate touch that made Heather
shiver.

"I should never have let you go back to your cottage
the other night. I should have kept you with me until
morning. Until you realized that with me you can be as
wildly passionate as you want. I can handle you,
Heather. I can take all you have to give. I *need* what you
have to give."

She moaned with a wrenching sense of longing and
desire as he buried his face against her throat. Heated
moist kisses were strung down to the collar of the black
knit pullover she wore, and when that barrier was
reached Jake pushed his hands up under the garment at
her waist. A moment later he had it over her head and
lying in a small heap on the floor beside the bed. The
delicate scrap of a bra seemed to come apart under his
hands. Jake fit his palms to her breasts.

"You're so sleek in some places and so soft in others," he breathed.

Heather searched his tightly drawn face, knowing her
nipples were responding to the grazing action of his
palms. She could see the satisfaction in his eyes when
he felt the tautness in her.

Her tongue moistened her suddenly dry mouth.
"Jake, I think I'm afraid of you. I've never been afraid
of a man in my life."

"Was that why you left me at the altar this morning?"

"Yes." The answer was simple and painfully clear. For
the first time she admitted that basic truth. "I would be

afraid of any man who could manipulate me the way you did. It's only logical."

"Heather, I don't have your charm and your easy way with people. I go after what I want using different tactics. I don't have any choice. I couldn't risk losing you."

"Taking me like this won't tie me to you," she told him throatily, uncertain in her own mind of the truth of that statement, but needing to make some protest.

"We'll talk about the future in the morning." He bent his head to kiss the curve of her breast. "Take off my shirt, Heather. I want to feel your skin against mine. Please."

There was such unexpected need in his plea that Heather found herself obeying without even thinking about it. Her trembling fingers went to the buttons of his khaki shirt. He raised himself far enough from her to enable Heather to push the garment awkwardly off his shoulders, and then with a groan he lowered himself once more. The cloud of dark curling hair on his chest seemed to scorch her skin as he crushed her to him. He had a strange power to make her unbearably sensitive and he seemed to know it. Know it and use it.

With strong urgent movements Jake unfastened Heather's belt and the jeans she wore. He rolled to one side, pulling her with him until he could shove the clothing down over her hips. Her white satin panties, the ones that had been bought to wear with her wedding dress, came with them.

Wonder and flaming male desire flared in his eyes as Jake luxuriously moved his palm down the full length of her nude body. Heather found herself responding fiercely to that undisguised hunger. Her fingertips traced the pattern of Jake's chest hair to the point where it disappeared beneath his jeans, and she heard his growl of pleasure. It seemed as though it was the most satisfying sound in the world.

"Your fingers feel like little bits of fire on my skin. I love the way you touch me, Heather. And I want you to touch all of me." He released her to fumble with his own belt. The bed moved beneath Heather as Jake abruptly got to his feet and stepped out of both jeans and underwear in one lithe motion. Then he hesitated a moment beside the bed, looking down at her.

"Do you want me, Heather? Can you give me that much at least? I need you so much tonight."

"Do you, Jake?" She lay watching him beneath the veil of her lashes, hiding the agonized uncertainty she was feeling. There was no doubt about how her body reacted to him, but the element of fear she had identified earlier still existed. Heather had never felt anything resembling the complex state of passion and wariness she now experienced.

"Yes. Oh, God, *yes!*"

Mutely she opened her arms to him, unable to hide her own desire. He came back to her in a rush of strength and need that dazzled. In a fever she opened herself to him, parting her legs at his touch, lifting herself in silent pleading invitation.

The hard thrusting shaft of his masculinity was poised near the juncture of her thighs, but Jake made no move yet to take possession. Instead he kissed her deeply while his fingers moved between them.

"Oh, Jake!"

His intimate touch made her soften like molten gold. Jake moved his head to her shoulder and used his teeth with exquisite care.

"Touch me, Heather. The way I'm touching you. Please, honey. I need it so."

Tremulously she obeyed, her hands moving down the length of his back to the flat planes of his hips. Convulsively she clenched her fingers there and heard his muffled response. Encouraged, she stroked his thigh, finding the inner surface as he stiffened slightly. And then he was thrusting himself into her palm.

"Yes! Oh, Heather, I'm on fire for you."

He pushed himself through her fingers, seeking the more satisfying warmth and tightness of her body. Heather gasped as he probed the entrance to her throbbing feminine core. For an instant fear rose up to stifle her breath and send a wave of panic through her system.

"Heather, don't fight me. You can't fight me. It's too late." Suddenly he was overwhelming her body's instinctive protest, sheathing himself deeply inside and drinking the cry of excitement and fear from her lips.

Heather clung to him, her nails biting into his skin, her legs tightening around his. She had no other choice. It was as if, finally, after all these years of working and wondering and waiting, everything really was *right*.

That sense of rightness was not something she had ever expected to feel in a man's arms. She had never dreamed it could be satisfied in such a way. But this was the answer she had been seeking. She knew it in the very depths of her being without understanding it. The world narrowed down to a single brilliant focal point.

Tonight Jake Cavender was the only thing in her life that truly mattered.

He swept her into the powerful rhythm of his lovemaking, tuning her body's response to his. Her pulse leaped and the desire in her shimmered in reaction.

"Jake! Oh, Jake!"

"Let it happen, honey," he rasped. "Just let go and take me with you."

He sank his fingers deeply into the flesh of her buttocks and Heather cried aloud. Her whole body seemed to convulse. The next instant she was rippling with endless streams of satisfaction and pleasure. It was unlike anything she had ever known. She heard Jake's answering shout of release and exultation and then they were locked together in a world of shattering intimacy.

Long moments later it was the realization of that intense intimacy that drove Heather to stir in Jake's arms. She had never known that feeling of complete union with another human being. Her relationships in the past had all been carefully controlled. They had never been allowed to intrude on her most fundamental emotions. Strange that it had been the unleashing of those elemental passions that had left her open and vulnerable to Jake's overpowering seduction. She had been right to keep those passions reined for so many years.

Beside her, Jake opened his eyes. "I don't suppose this was the most conventional wedding night on record, but then I had a feeling you weren't going to be a very conventional sort of bride. In spite of your usually charming personality."

She searched his face, seeing the relaxed humor in him along with the deep masculine satisfaction. She had achieved that, Heather found herself thinking. She had brought him that satisfaction. Whatever pleasure and fulfillment he had given her; she had provided equal value. A good team.

"What's wrong?" Jake propped himself up on his elbow, concern shadowing his gaze. He touched the corner of her mouth with his thumb. "What are you thinking, Heather? A moment ago you were feeling as good as I did."

"I was thinking about how everyone says we make such a great team."

"Ah. You were applying that phrase to our current situation, is that it?" A grin tugged at his mouth; the first real grin Heather had ever seen on him. "I'm inclined to agree. We make a fantastic team in bed. But I knew we would."

"It's not funny, Jake."

He sobered. "You're still afraid, aren't you? Afraid of what we have together."

She lowered her eyes, not wanting to admit either that she still knew fear or that they really had found something unique together. But his forefinger lifted her chin, forcing her to meet his gaze.

"We are a good team, Heather. And as far as I'm concerned, tonight was our wedding night. We belong to each other now."

She moved her head restlessly, desperate to refute his words for some reason she couldn't fully explain. "One night in bed changes nothing."

"It changes everything."

"You really are used to getting what you want, aren't you?" she whispered.

"I think we're both accustomed to working hard for what we want. And we're both used to reaching our goals. Don't accuse me of arrogance, honey, unless you're willing to apply the same label to yourself."

"Whatever arrogance I had is gone. You've made me realize just how weak and manipulatable I really am. Except for that scene at the chapel this morning you've been able to handle me as if I were clay."

His face hardened. "Heather, listen to me...."

"I suppose it's rather amusing on some levels. After all, I'm the one who's supposed to be so good at handling people. It looks as though your methods are more successful than my so-called charm, doesn't it?"

"Hush, honey. You don't know what you're saying." Jake brushed her lips with the tips of his fingers. "Once we get a few of the details ironed out, you and I are going to be a perfect team. Just as everyone says."

Heather took a deep breath. "I don't think I want to be part of the team."

His gaze narrowed. "You don't have a whole lot of choice anymore."

"Yes, I do," she managed with a resurgence of pride. "I told you earlier that this night would be on my terms. It's not a wedding night, Jake."

His hand tightened abruptly at the curve of her shoulder. "Then call it a night of surrender. Your surrender. If you have to spell it out, so be it!"

He moved, forcing her deeply in the bedclothes as his hardening body came down on hers. Her skin, still damp from their previous encounter, came alive under his bold touch.

Heather cried out softly, half in protest and half in surrender, and then she was once more swept away by the passion that flowed between herself and Jake.

HOURS LATER HEATHER WOKE to find herself curled closely up to Jake's warm body. The quiet hum of the air-conditioning unit was the only sound that reached her besides the occasional passing car. It was past midnight, almost two in the morning. She had been held in the grip of shared desire and the shared exhaustion of the aftermath for almost a whole night.

Her wedding night, she thought bleakly. No, her night of surrender. Jake had been right on that score. She had given herself completely, glorying in the satisfaction of pleasing him, allowing herself the exquisite happiness of being pleased by him. *Allowing* was not the correct word, she acknowledged as she stared into the darkness. Accepting, welcoming, craving, hungering. Those were far more appropriate descriptors.

She had lost her head yesterday morning and she'd lost herself that night.

Lying here in the shadows of the passion-rumpled bed, Heather faced the reality of what had happened to her. Her rage yesterday morning had stemmed from more than just the fact that she'd been outmaneuvered. She'd felt betrayed on some level even though logic told her she had no one to blame but herself.

Jake was right when he'd claimed she was every bit as arrogant if not more so than he was. She'd come back to Tucson on her own terms, she'd said. But it was devastatingly clear to her that the only way she could stay would be on Jake's.

And now she had to deal with what it all meant. The kind of betrayal she had felt and the knowledge that her pride had been overcome by Jake's sensual assault were suddenly matters of paramount importance. Never had she allowed a man to play such havoc with her mind and body. She had to confront the fact that Jake had power over her. Only one explanation accounted for that power.

She had fallen in love with Jake Cavender.

A frisson of genuine fear tingled through her veins. She was vulnerable. Vulnerable to a man. Somehow she had never imagined that being in love left a woman in such an emotional tangle. Shaken by the realization of what had happened to her, she was unaware that Jake was awake until he moved slightly beside her.

"Heather?" His voice as thick as a sleepy lion's, Jake moved his face into her tousled hair. "Go back to sleep, honey."

She shook her head and then realized he couldn't see the negative gesture. He felt it, however.

"What is it, Heather?"

"My parents," she whispered, reluctant to tell him the truth about what she had really been thinking. "I have to call them. After what I did yesterday..."

"Don't worry about your parents. I told them I'd bring you home in a few days."

She turned her head on the pillow, seeking his eyes in the shadowy light. "Jake...."

"I also told them why you ran. That you must have found out about the sale of the Hacienda. If it's any consolation, your mother was on your side. She was absolutely furious."

"But she always supports my father!" Heather exclaimed, shocked.

"She didn't this time. She read the riot act to Paul and me. And then I told her I'd find you and bring you home."

Bring you home. Heather felt a wave of panic at his cool words. She wasn't ready to go home, she thought frantically. She needed time to assimilate the impact of the emotional assault she had experienced. She needed time to deal with the knowledge that she had fallen in love. A woman deserved the right to adjust to such a disorienting sequence of events in her own way, Heather told herself forcefully. Time to regain her composure and her thoughts. Time to understand the full potential of the radical twist her life had taken.

"It's not that simple," she whispered.

"It is if you'll let it be."

"Jake, I need some time to myself. Time to think. You've turned my whole world upside down."

"We're even, then."

"No. Your world is all neatly organized, humming along exactly as you planned. I want some time to reorganize my own world. Some time by myself."

"How much time?" he asked harshly.

"I don't know. A few days. Maybe longer. Maybe much longer."

"Heather, you belong to me now. You know that."

"Do I?" she challenged huskily, unwilling to give him that final verbal victory.

He hesitated as if deciding how to deal with her and then he ignored the challenge and asked softly, "Where will you go?"

"Into the hills, I think. My father has an old hunting cabin up in one of the canyons. It's isolated; totally away from everything. When I come back I'll know what I'm going to do."

"I don't want you to go, Heather." There was a thread of command in the words.

"I have to go," she told him flatly. "I have to think it all through."

"Trust me, honey. Everything's going to be fine."

"At the moment I can't even trust myself," she murmured.

Jake watched her shadowed face and knew that he would have to let her go for the moment. He'd taken her world apart and he told himself she had a right to figure out whether or not she wanted the new one he was offering.

It was a gamble. The biggest risk he'd taken in a lifetime full of risks. Separated from him she might succeed in arguing away the bonds that he had tried to put in place tonight. Given enough time she might be able to tell herself that she didn't need him or the Hacienda or her family's approval. After all, she'd survived without any of those factors for years. But he'd taken so much. He owed some respect to the proud spirit he'd tried to chain.

"In the morning, Heather. I'll let you go in the morning," he grated roughly. "Grant me what's left of my wedding night!" He pulled her into his arms and she came to him in soft sensual obedience.

"YOU CAN TAKE THE CAR," Jake said quietly the next morning after they had risen and dressed and shared a cup of coffee in the motel restaurant. He dug the keys out of his pocket.

Heather accepted them uncertainly. "How will you get home . . . I mean, how will you get back to the Hacienda?"

"I'll drive poor Jim's motorcycle." Jake's mouth slanted wryly. "The kid must be out of his mind with worry by now."

"The bike?" She eyed him in surprise. "Do you . . . that is, can you, uh, ride it?"

"I'll manage."

"I see. Well, I guess I'll have to stop and get a few things when the stores open," Heather went on uneasily. She felt tense and high-strung this morning. Jake seemed to be overflowing with understanding. For some reason that irritated her.

"If you're talking about clothing, there's a suitcase in the back of the Mercedes. Your mother packed it for you so it should have everything you need."

She stared at him in astonishment. "I see," she finally said again.

"I doubt it but I'm hoping you will after you've had your time alone." He stood up and negligently threw some cash onto the table. "We'd better get going."

Fifteen minutes later Heather turned the key in the Mercedes, watching through the side window as Jake expertly fired up the motorcycle and swung his booted foot over the seat. He gave her a sidelong glance as he stood bracing the growling monster with one foot on the ground.

"A few days, Heather," he reminded her over the muted roar. "That's all."

She nodded and put the Mercedes in gear. As she did so, Jake let the motorcycle have its way, guiding it out of the parking lot with a touch that spoke volumes in terms of experience. The man definitely knew what he was doing on a motorcycle and that thought intrigued Heather. She wanted to know where and when he'd learned to ride with that kind of casual expertise.

As he disappeared down the road she noticed something and frowned in sudden consternation. "Jake, the helmet! You forgot to put on the helmet!"

But he was well out of earshot.

And this was the man who had given Jim Connors a safety lecture, she remembered in disgust. Then Heather grinned. Perhaps he was the kind of rider who would stop as soon as he was out of sight and put on the helmet, just as she always did. It was one thing to leave an impression of reckless grit and glory on one's audience, quite another to actually tempt suicide!

The small grin stayed with Heather as she automatically tuned in a country-and-western channel on the Mercedes's radio. It was strange how she was so certain that Jake would put on the helmet after he'd ridden out of sight. It was as if she knew how he would react this morning because she knew he was similar to her in many ways.

That thought wiped away the smile. What an idiotic assumption to make on the basis of one night together. She must be out of her mind.

She wasn't out of her mind; she was in love. A much more serious state of affairs. A steel guitar and the laconic complaint of a cowboy who was drinking to get a woman out of his mind echoed around the front seat of the Mercedes. Heather found herself wondering if Jake could ever be reduced to such a condition.

Stretching a little in the driver's seat, Heather became wryly aware of the small sensual aches in her body. Jake's lovemaking had left her vividly aware of him in several places, Heather reflected grimly. But the unanswered question had to do with the effect she'd had on Jake.

He wanted her. In some sense he needed her. She was the key to making his carefully constructed home perfect. By marrying her, Jake would be securing his position in the minds and hearts of both the Strand family and the Hacienda staff. He would become a genuine part of the crowd of successful businesspeople Paul Strand had mingled with here in Tucson. He would preserve the heritage of having a Strand intimately involved with the running of the hotel. That would please Heather's father greatly.

Yes, Jake needed her, Heather thought. And he wanted her. He had proven that beyond a doubt last night. Furthermore, it had been as much her idea to marry for convenience as it had been his. What was the matter with her this morning? Nothing had really changed. It was true that it had been a shock to discover she was not going to inherit the Hacienda, but she had adjusted to that yesterday.

Perhaps what she hadn't adjusted to was the sense of betrayal. Yet she knew Jake was offering her a position almost identical to the one she had thought lost. Not quite identical, of course. Jake Cavender would always have final responsibility for the fate of the Hacienda. But she could be a part of it if she wished. All she had to do was marry him. Her goals of coming home to make things "right"; to settle back into the life-style of the Hacienda Strand and its environs, could still be obtained.

All she had to do was marry Jake Cavender—just as she had planned.

It was with a sense of astonishment that Heather finally acknowledged the real problem this morning. She had fallen in love with Jake and quite suddenly she no longer wanted to be married for business reasons. Heather shook her head wryly as she guided the Mercedes along the highway that led into the hills where her father's cabin was located. Jake had done more than compel her physical and emotional surrender last night. He had succeeded in reviving the passionate outlook on life that she had subdued so successfully for the past few years. Marrying for convenience or for business reasons, no matter how satisfactory to all parties concerned, was simply no longer good enough.

When she turned off the road it was to take the much narrower, less-used trail that led into the canyon Heather remembered so well. The desert terrain gave way a bit to scruffy shrubs and trees. The stately saguaro cacti were prevalent, their candelabra configurations lending elegance to the surroundings. The road was not paved and Heather slowed the Mercedes to avoid raising any more dust than was necessary.

It was going to be hot at the cabin. There was no air conditioning and not much else in the way of ameni-

ties. Heather wondered what her mother had thought
when Paul had brought her up here on their honeymoon. At lest Ruth had known she was being married
for love and not for convenience. Heather sighed,
slowing the car still further.

The cabin was showing its years and lack of attention. It sat perched several yards from a stream that
cascaded down out of the mountains, its wood gray
with age. The roof tilted rather precariously and one
of the front windows had been broken. Heather parked
the Mercedes and climbed out to survey the scene of
some of her childhood memories. Even though Paul
Strand had given up hunting years ago, the family had
continued to use the cabin for picnics in the summer.
The cool stream, swollen from the recent rains, was an
inviting place in which to swim, and the canyon had
provided fascinating places to explore. There were even
some caves tucked into the walls upstream, Heather
remembered.

The cabin didn't have electricity, but there was running water. Heather, when she tested the rusty faucet
in the small kitchen area, was astonished to find that it
still worked. With any luck the bathroom facilities
would, also. No hot water, of course, but she could live
without it for a couple of days.

A couple of days. As she prowled the environs of the
one-room cabin, Heather considered the time factor
Jake had placed on this retreat. He had seemed to sense
that she needed the time to collect her thoughts and
come to her own decisions. He'd let her go this morning with hardly any argument.

For some reason that lack of argument was making her uneasy. It didn't seem to fit his character. He must have known how thorough her surrender had been last night. Indeed, he'd reveled in it. Heather grimaced.

But knowing that, and knowing him, it seemed far more likely that he would be the kind of man to press the advantage. Yet this morning he'd casually bought her a cup of coffee and waved her on her way.

Not like him at all.

Heather prodded the dusty, half-collapsed couch under the broken window. It was damp from rain that had made its way down the inside wall of the cabin. There were some floorboards loose, too. Experimentally she stepped on one, listening to the protesting squeak.

Visions of Jake changing his mind and coming after her danced through Heather's head. The romantic passionate side of her that had been freed by the emotional trauma of the past twenty-four hours longed for such an event. The realistic side of her nature warned her that nothing would be changed by such an occurrence. She would still be faced with the decision she faced now.

She must decide what she truly wanted out of life, and that decision could not be made the way she had made it when she was eighteen. It had to be made logically and realistically when you knew you were in love.

She ought to be thinking about the manner in which she'd lost her right to the Hacienda, Heather told herself grimly as she went out to the Mercedes and removed the suitcase her mother had packed. She ought to be concentrating on the sense of betrayal she had felt yesterday. But that red-hot emotion was no longer one she could tap into easily. Jake had cooled it, replacing it with his claim on her. The desire to satisfy his physical and emotional needs had quickly become paramount last night.

She had her own needs, however, Heather reminded herself as she carried the suitcase into the cabin and opened it. A piece of her mother's stationery lay on top of the neatly arranged pile of underwear and assorted clothing.

My dearest Heather,

As usual, our best-laid plans for you have gone awry. But this time you have my full backing. The nerve of those two men keeping the news about the sale of the Hacienda from us! I was furious on your behalf. I have no objections to Jake owning the place. And I'm glad Paul has finally decided to retire. But you should have been told exactly what the situation was! I know you and Jake will eventually work out your problems. He's a good man, dear. But I think you have every right to marry him on your own terms.

All my love, Mother.

Tears burned for a few seconds behind Heather's eyes. Hastily she dashed them away with the back of her hand. And then she carefully folded the note. Her mother's understanding only succeeded in making her feel worse about the scene she had caused yesterday.

On the other hand, Heather told herself unhappily, there weren't a great many polite ways to leave a man standing alone at the altar. She swallowed a sigh and rummaged around in the suitcase until she found some fresh underwear and a persimmon-colored shirt. Her mother had thoughtfully packed a pair of rubber-soled shoes, too, which would be cooler than the leather boots she was wearing.

Heather quickly changed clothes and refastened the designer jeans. Then she set about taking her mind off her problems by concentrating on the business of starting a fire in the old cook stove. Having stopped to pick up some canned goods before leaving Tucson, she knew she wasn't going to starve.

Overhead the clouds began to form for the afternoon thunderstorms. Huge billowing masses of unstable air whirled in the sky, darkening vast areas of desert and mountain. Her father, Heather remembered, had said the rains were unusually heavy this year. She hoped the cabin didn't have too many holes in its old roof.

The distant sounds of approaching thunder hid the noise of the car until it was already in the cabin's driveway. When the engine growl did register, Heather leaped to her feet, torn between anticipation and uncertainty.

Jake had come after her.

In that moment of tension and excitement Heather told herself that she had known all along he would change his mind. He wasn't the kind of man to risk having her talk herself out of the commitment she had made last night.

Right, wrong or impossible, Heather knew a fierce gladness as she threw open the cabin door.

But the car that had parked in front of the old place was not one she recognized. It was a covered jeep, and as the driver slowly emerged all of Heather's anticipation and excitement disappeared in a flash. There was a gun in the hand of the man who climbed so coolly out of the jeep.

Heather stared in shock, her attention so completely on the menacing weapon in the man's hand that she didn't even glance at the face for several seconds. She stood braced in the doorway and frantically wondered if she could duck back inside and slam the door shut before the stranger could fire.

"Well, hell," the intruder muttered softly. "I don't believe it. It is Heather Strand, isn't it?"

She jerked her eyes up to meet the laconic, dark-eyed gaze of the stranger. Desperately she struggled to make her voice sound controlled. "Yes, I'm Heather Strand. My family owns this cabin."

"Don't you think I know that? Small world, isn't it? How have you been Heather? I've often wondered whether or not you made it big in California."

"Oh, my God. You're Rick, aren't you?" The black hair was thinning rapidly and there was a definite paunch around his waist, but the dark eyes that had once seemed so captivating were the same. "I...I didn't recognize you."

"Are you alone?"

"Yes. Yes, I just came up for a couple of days," she explained cautiously.

"A couple of days. Just like old times, hmm? Remember when you and I used to ride that bike of yours up here to spend the afternoon?"

"I remember." Her eyes went back to the gun. "What are you doing here, Rick?"

He followed her gaze down to the weapon in his hand and chuckled. Then he stuck the ugly object into his belt. "Me? I come up here a lot, Heather. Your father hasn't used this place since you were in high school."

"I know that."

"Personally, I've always had a soft spot in my heart for the old cabin." He reached into the jeep and yanked the keys out of the ignition. Dropping them into his pocket he started forward. "Lots of nice memories. What about you, Heather? Do you ever think of the plans we came up here to make?"

"I haven't thought of those plans since the day you ripped off my motorcycle and left me standing in the middle of the desert." She held her ground as long as possible in the doorway, but when he was a step away and showing every sign of pushing past her, Heather stepped back into the cabin. "Why the gun, Rick?"

"You never know who you're going to run into out here in the middle of nowhere," he said lazily, stepping inside the cabin and glancing around. Thunder cracked overhead as the sky continued to darken. "Looks like we're in for a bad one this afternoon. That stream outside is already full. A heavy shower could send it over the banks. Not a good day to pick to relive old memories, Heather." He swung around to face her.

Heather looked at the man with whom she'd fled Tucson so many years ago and thanked her lucky stars that he'd left her standing alongside that desert highway. How could she have possibly once considered linking her life with this man? The dark good looks had faded now and there had been nothing of character or strength to replace them. Rick was only in his midthirties but everything about him seemed to have thickened and coarsened. It was not simply that he had put on weight, but it seemed as if the potential for earthy sensuality he once possessed had degenerated into unappealing vulgarity. As if the spirit of rebellion that had first attracted her to him had turned into something ignoble and sly. Uneasily Heather fingered the keys to the Mercedes that were in the pocket of her jeans. She found herself wanting to be well away from Rick Monroe.

"I didn't come up here to relive old memories, Rick. I'm here to spend a few quiet days by myself. Why are you here?"

"Me?" He finished circling the cabin, having stopped to glance into the small bath, and sat down on an overstuffed arm of the old sofa. "Well, Heather, I'm afraid I'm here on business."

"Business?"

He grinned unpleasantly. "I'm a businessman now. Bet you never thought I'd be successful without your father's money, did you? I still remember how you chewed me out that day we left Tucson when you found out I wanted you to call home for money. You were so set on showing everyone you could make it on your own. Personally, I never saw the need to do things the hard way."

"So how have you been doing things?" she challenged tightly, not liking the tension in the atmosphere.

"Profitably." He nodded as if to himself. "Profitably, thank you. Of course, I won't be playing golf at your father's club and I don't take vacations in and around Tucson. I try to stay away from old acquaintances. No sense being asked a lot of stupid questions."

"Questions like the ones I'm asking?"

His mouth quirked. "Yeah. Questions like those."

Angrily Heather moved to the window, not taking her eyes off Rick. "If you make it a point not to hang around old acquaintances, why are you hanging around this cabin?"

"I use this place, Heather. I guess you could say it's my corporate headquarters." He eyed his surroundings derisively. "I think it all has a kind of poetic justice."

"What does?"

"Me using Strand property to found my own personal empire."

"Rick, you're not making any sense. And I think you may be right about that stream. It is running higher than usual, even for this time of the year. If we get a lot more rain this afternoon, it could overflow and block the road. I think I'm going to change my mind about staying here."

Determinedly Heather walked to the door. Her instincts were clamoring, warning her to put as much distance as possible between herself and Rick Monroe. She decided to forget about the suitcase her mother had so carefully packed.

"Enjoy yourself, Rick. I'm going to leave you alone in your 'corporate headquarters.'"

Her hand was on the old glass doorknob when he spoke behind her. Even before she turned around she knew she would see the gun in his grip.

"I'm afraid I can't let you waltz out of here, sweetheart. I've got an important meeting of the board this evening and I'd kinda like you to attend. Be a real education for you."

"Forget it." But she couldn't forget the gun and they both knew it.

"Sit down, Heather. Let's talk about old times."

"I don't think we have anything to say to each other, Rick." She tried to face him down. Eleven years ago she had been able to handle him. But eleven years ago he'd been anxious to keep her happy.

"We've got lots to talk about, Heather. I just know you're dying of curiosity. Want to know how rich I am? I'm worth nearly half a million right at this moment. By the time tonight's business is finished, I'll be worth almost three-quarters of a mil. I've learned to think big, baby. A lot bigger than I did in the old days."

"I don't want any part of your schemes. Get rich on your own and leave me out of it," she hissed.

He made a show of putting the gun back into his belt. "You've made yourself a part of my plans, Heather." He rose and moved toward her. "But if you do exactly as you're told I think we might get along okay, after all. Course things will be different this time around. As I recall you were always a bossy sort of kid. And something tells me you probably turned into a bossy sort of woman. Just remember that I run this show and there's every possibility we might work out. How about that,

Heather? Think you might like finding out what you missed when you told me to get lost eleven years ago?"

"No."

"You aren't going to have much choice, sweetheart. Not much choice at all."

Before she could respond the thunder cracked again overhead. Heather found herself chewing on her lower lip, her fingers thrust into the front pockets of her jeans. She was scared and she didn't dare show it. Not to this man. He'd take far too much pleasure in the knowledge.

"Look, Rick. You and I went in two different directions all those years ago. I don't think either one of us really wants to find out where the other's been for the past few years. Let's just forget the reunion. You stay here and do your thing and I'll go back to Tucson and do mine."

He chuckled rudely. "Come on, now Heather. You know it's not going to be that simple, don't you?"

Heather was trying to think of a cool way to handle the menacing question when the sound of another car approaching the cabin was heard. She wasn't certain at first if it was another vehicle because the heavens chose that moment to send down the first sheets of water.

A scowl appeared on Rick's heavy features and he glanced at his watch. "I told him not to come until after dark. He's hours early, the fool!" He leaped to his feet, propelling Heather aside with a shove. The angry look on his face intensified as he peered out the broken window. Then Rick swore violently.

"The damn place is turning into a parking lot! You know that guy?" He jerked back from the window, reaching out to grab Heather's arm and yank her forward.

Somehow Heather knew who she would see getting out of the white Fiat. The car was her mother's but the man getting ready to make a hurried dash to the poor protection of the small porch was Jake Cavender.

He had come after her; just as she'd known he would. Because of her he would be walking into Rick's gun.

"I'll get rid of him," she rasped pleadingly as she swung her head around to face a nervous and glowering Rick. "Just give me a chance. I'll make him go away. He's here because of me."

"What the hell's going on? You two going to shack up here or something?"

"Just let me have a chance to get rid of him, Rick. Please. If you do I'll cooperate with you. I swear I won't give you any trouble."

"What are you going to do? Tell him you came up here to meet me instead of him?" Rick mocked furiously.

"Why not?" Her eyes burned into his. Heather tried to summon whatever degree of willpower she had ever possessed and used it on Monroe. "It will be easier for you if he goes away quietly."

Rick hesitated, clearly torn. He glanced out the window one more time and his dark gaze narrowed. "Yeah, I like it. I really like it. Okay, babe, let's see you convince this guy you came all this way to jump in the sack with me. But if it doesn't work, he's dead. You got me?"

Heather swallowed. "I understand."

7

HE LOOKED SO GOOD coming toward her through the rain. Heather's heart turned over as she took in the sight of Jake dodging quickly around the small rivulets of water that were already beginning to run over the unabsorbent ground. He was still wearing jeans and low-cut desert boots. The shirt was fresh, though; a dark, long-sleeved one with the collar open. His teak-shaded hair was very wet by the time he reached the rickety porch, and Heather watched longingly through the window as he ran a hand through it.

She saw him glance at the unfamiliar car in the drive and when he turned to pound on the door his eyes were cool and wary. A month ago Heather knew she would not have been able to interpret that gaze beyond those limits.

But his lifted hand paused and fell back to his side as he caught sight of her staring at him through the broken glass, and Heather was suddenly certain she could read a lot more than remote caution in him. There was determination and concern and a familiar intentness that told her as well as any words that he had come to take her home.

"Heather, for God's sake, let me in. It's pouring out here in case you haven't noticed."

She turned away from the window, her limbs feeling as though they were weighted with lead. The expression on Rick's face was chillingly sardonic, but there was an underlying nervous tension in him that made her doubly wary. She saw him stuff the gun under a couch cushion and then fling himself casually down beside it.

"Let the man inside, babe. Let's see how good an actress you turned out to be. There was always a bit of the dramatic in you, wasn't there?" He patted the cushion that shielded the gun. "And just in case you aren't up to academy level today, I'll have this little backup waiting."

Her heart pounding, Heather opened the door, stepping back silently as Jake came into the room. His eyes went fleetingly over her mask of a face and then he focused on Rick Monroe.

"What are you doing here, Jake?" Heather wrapped her arms across her breasts in an unconscious hug similar to the one she often used when under great stress. The last time she had braced herself like this was when Jake had confronted her in the motel room in Tucson.

"I should think the answer to that question is obvious." Jake flicked a sidelong glance at her, dark brows forming a near-solid line over his narrowed eyes. "I came to take you back."

He must never know just how badly she wanted to go with him. Grimly Heather drew a breath and gathered her courage. Jake's life depended on how well she handled the next few minutes. Above all else she must keep him safe. She might be able to take care of Monroe on her own because of their relationship so many years ago, but Jake wouldn't have a chance against Rick's gun.

"Then I'm afraid you've wasted your time, Jake." She flashed a meaningful glance at Monroe. "As you can see, I've got company."

Monroe gave Jake a challenging look. "Why don't you tell your visitor who I am, babe?"

"Jake, this is Rick Monroe." If Jake recognized the name, and she knew he must have, he gave no sign. Desperately Heather sought for the next words. "Rick and I are old friends." She tried to stress the word *friends* in a way that would imply a double meaning.

"I see." Jake stared at the other man, every line in his lean frame hard and poised as if to attack. "You didn't mention you expected to have old *friends* visiting up here with you, Heather."

Heather's mouth went dry. Jake was frighteningly angry. She knew it as plainly as if he'd threatened violence. But for some reason she didn't think Rick Monroe sensed the other man's fury.

"Rick and I used to spend a lot of time up here at this old cabin," she said hastily, knowing she had to get him out of here for his sake.

"A lot of time," Rick concurred. "A lot of interesting time. We didn't especially appreciate visitors then and we don't like 'em any better now, do we, babe?"

"No. No, we don't. Jake, I told you in Tucson that everything was over between us. Why did you follow me? Can't you see that it makes things a little awkward, to say the least?"

Jake swung around to confront her, turning his back to Monroe. "Suppose you explain this awkward little situation a bit more clearly," he bit out. "I'd like to hear the details."

Heather lifted her head instinctively at the sound of the cold demand in him. Vaguely astonished that even in this extreme sort of situation her rebelliousness could surface, Heather glared at him. She could use that natural reaction to save his arrogant neck, she told herself. "Oh, come now, Jake. I'm sure you don't want to hear all the details. Take my word for it, Rick and I have a lot to discuss. It's been a long time, hasn't it, Rick?"

"Yeah."

"And we're rather anxious to get on with the, uh, reunion."

"You expect me to just walk out that door and drive back to Tucson?" Jake inquired far too softly.

Heather shivered and moved a little restlessly, but she kept her eyes level and her chin arrogantly high. "That's just exactly what I expect. I'm really not into the ménage à trois scene."

Jake's mouth tightened and his eyes blazed for an instant. In that moment Heather was desperately afraid he would give way to the fury that she sensed was eating him alive. Frantically she sought for further words. Anything to get rid of him.

"Hey, let's skip the foreign lingo unless it's Spanish," Rick warned from across the room. His hand hovered just above the cushion concealing the gun.

"Jake, will you please go?" Heather muttered, wrenching her gaze away from his accusing eyes. "Just get out of here. Can't you see you're not wanted? Rick and I go back a long way together. We were always attracted to each other." She stumbled awkwardly over the word *attracted*. She should have said that she and Rick had been lovers, but it had been impossible to get the lie out of her mouth.

"Yeah, we got this strong mutual *attraction*," Rick mocked. "In other words, we're real compatible in bed."

Jake ignored him. Heather was the whole focus of his shatteringly intent regard. "And what about us?" he asked her quietly. "What about last night?"

It was then Heather realized she could never make him believe a complete lie. If she was now able to read him more accurately, then she had to assume the relationship worked both ways. He would be able to perceive that she was lying. Perhaps she could make him understand the situation was highly dangerous by the very fact that she was forced to such extremes. He was brilliant in business. It remained to be seen just how brilliant he was at reading her mind. She dug her nails into her arms as she continued to hold herself.

"Last night was amusing, Jake." She managed a fleeting wry smile. "Or at least it was from my point of view. I hope you didn't make any more out of it than an interesting toss in the hay. I thought I made my own feelings toward you quite clear at the time. I was under the impression you understood exactly how I felt."

"And I thought you understood exactly how I felt," he countered evenly.

"Yes, well, men often say things they don't mean in the heat of passion. So do women. Let's just call the whole thing a learning experience, shall we? Now, if you don't mind, I'd like you to go." She continued looking at him, her gaze unwavering. She did want him to go, for his own sake. "Please go away and leave me alone. I'm tired of the way you've been pestering me for the past few weeks. I'm tired of discussing business with you. Always business. That's all you ever want to talk about. You know I couldn't care less about that damn hotel. Or about you."

"I didn't realize how completely bored you were in my company," Jake said silkily.

"Yes, well, I tried to be polite for my parents' sake, but to tell you the truth, I get incredibly tired of hearing about nothing except plans for the Hacienda every time I come home to visit. You're as bad as Dad is about that place. No wonder I left for California when I was eighteen. The thought of taking over Dad's position was very unpleasant."

"I'm the one she left town with that day," Monroe said pleasantly.

Jake glanced at him over his shoulder, his scorn barely under control. "Were you?"

"Yup. So you can see just how far back Heather and I go. A real close attachment."

For a second Heather thought Rick's brash need to assert himself in front of the other man had pushed Jake too far. But then Jake turned back to her, gray eyes quite unreadable.

"It looks like you've made your choice, Heather."

"Yes." She tried to keep her face expressionless. "I'm sorry if you're a bit disappointed, but I'm sure you've learned to accept rejection before. I'm really not interested in what you're offering, Jake. I couldn't care less about creating a home and putting down roots. I've been living in California for the past few years, remember? You get used to being on the cutting edge out there. It gets in your blood. The idea of settling down in Tucson for the rest of my life is enough to scare the daylights out of me. I appreciate your nice offer but I really can't accept. Go find yourself some nice female who wants to bake bread and make babies. I'm sure you'll be much happier with someone like that than you'd ever be with me. I'd drive you crazy and we both know it."

To her surprise he nodded in agreement. "You may be right. About driving me crazy, I mean. Well, I can see when I'm not wanted. I'm sorry I bothered you, Heather. I really thought we had found something together. Something important." He stopped as if inviting her to change her mind.

"Nothing I can't live without," she said flippantly, although her heart was breaking. It seemed that only as she went through the charade of rejecting him did she realize just how much he meant to her.

"Goodbye, Heather. I won't annoy you and your *friend* any further. You know I'm not the kind of man who hangs around when he's not wanted. I like to think I'm a gentleman."

Heather blinked. A gentleman? No gentleman would have tracked her down to that motel and seduced her the way Jake had done last night. No gentleman would have deliberately lured her into marriage by concealing the true financial facts of the situation. It occurred to Heather that Jake Cavender was definitely not a gentleman. He was a street fighter.

But he was handling this situation as if he was an impeccably behaved, well-mannered gentleman struggling to rise above an embarrassing event.

"You know I have no doubts on that score," Heather murmured coolly. "It's just that true gentlemen tend to be so dull."

Jake stood very still, and then without glancing back at a sneering Rick Monroe, he strode to the door. Flinging it open he stalked out into the rain and went to the car. A moment later the Fiat roared to life. Heather stood at the window, watching as the man she loved drove off into the storm.

"Well, well, well. You've really gotten to be a tough little broad over the past few years, haven't you?" Monroe got to his feet, ambling over to where Heather stood staring out into the gathering darkness. He lifted a hand and traced a line down her cheek and along her shoulder. The sickening sensuality of the gesture made Heather flinch.

She covered the reaction by stepping away. "What happens now, Rick?"

"We wait."

"For what?"

"The arrival of my partner. It's going to be a while. I got here early because I've found that partners in my line of work have a nasty habit of double-crossing each other. Safest to arrive early at the scene of a meeting. Not that I have any reason to be suspicious of Joe. He's a pretty good guy, all things considered. And we've worked together before."

"Doing what?"

"You really want to know?" he drawled.

"No, I don't think so," Heather gritted. "Something tells me that the less I know the better."

"You sure kept that joker in the Fiat from guessing anything at all. I was impressed. Like I said, you're tough. Had a lot of experience tossing men aside?"

Something new in the tone of his voice warned Heather that matters had taken a turn toward the more dangerous. Assuming it was possible for things to get worse.

"I don't imagine you're particularly interested in the status of my love life," she tried mildly.

"Oh, I don't know. The way you handled that guy a few minutes ago reminded me a little of the way you told me to go to hell that day we left Tucson. And he went. Just like I did."

"At least he didn't steal my transportation in the process!"

"Maybe not, but he sure managed to leave you stranded, didn't he?" Rick retorted in savage amusement. "You must have really wanted to get rid of him. Why was that, Heather? Because he is as dull as you told him he was or because you were trying to protect him?"

"Both. He's a nice guy, Rick. I don't want him involved."

"A nice guy," Monroe repeated. "You know what they say about nice guys."

"You don't seem to have had much experience along that line yourself."

"Nah, I'm not a nice guy. But then, I never was. If I had been, you wouldn't have wanted to run off with me when you were eighteen."

"I wanted to run off with you because I thought you were a lot like me," Heather whispered, walking tensely to the window. The Fiat and its driver were long gone. Heather felt more alone than she had ever felt in her life. She could only hope and pray that she'd managed to communicate to Jake the fact that something was drastically wrong. But even if he'd picked up her message there wasn't much time for him to drive all the way back into town and call for help. The rain was pounding down into the canyon at a steadily increasing rate. The force of this evening's storms was bound to make driving all but impossible for long stretches.

Then there was the other, more probable situation. Jake might not have realized she was in any kind of trouble at all. Perhaps he really had taken his rejection like a gentleman.

No matter how hard Heather tried to convince herself that was the case, she couldn't quite do it. A man who had schemed to get her to the altar so that he could lock in everything in life that was important to him; a man who hadn't taken the rejection of being abandoned at that altar and had chased down his bride to claim his wedding night; a man like that wouldn't just meekly walk out of a situation like this. Surely he wouldn't simply abandon the woman he'd worked so hard to possess.

Unless he'd come to the conclusion that he didn't want her after last night.

"Why don't you fix us some coffee, Heather? And feed that fire a bit. It's getting cool in here. Geez, there's a lot of water coming down out there."

"What will you do if your business partner can't make it up that road?" Almost grateful for a task to give her something to do, Heather set about making coffee in an old pot. Her father had taught her how to do it over a cook stove. His recipe made for a brew that would probably float spoons.

As she searched through the drawers, looking for old dishes, she was surprised to come across a cabinet full of reasonably new mugs, canned coffee and other miscellaneous items.

"I put all that stuff in there," Rick commented as he saw her looking at the contents of the cabinet. "I told you I use this place a lot."

"Where did you go after you took the bike and left me standing alongside the highway, Rick?" She would try to keep matters as casual as possible; pretend they really were old friends rehashing the past. And perhaps while she worked she'd find some item that could be used as a weapon.

"Let's see," the man mused, never taking his eyes off her. "I went on to Los Angeles. A bright guy with an expensive bike to sell can get a good start in a city like that. I used that motorcycle as capital, you might say. Made some investments."

"Investments!" She looked up, startled.

"Drugs, babe." He grinned at her naiveté, shaking his head. "For all your free-spirited talk back in the old days, you were real straight, weren't you?"

"I didn't realize it bothered you," she retorted caustically. "You sure made it a point to hang around me a lot."

He shrugged, his fingers idly toying with the handle of the gun he'd recovered from under the cushion and thrust back into his belt. It was another small gesture of nervous tension and it made Heather more nervous.

"I figured that what I'd be able to collect from your old man would make it worth putting up with your crazy notions of right and wrong. You couldn't have been more off base in thinking that you and I had a lot in common," he taunted.

"I found that out as soon as I made it clear I would not be contacting my father for money the day we left town."

"You made such a scene that day." Rick shook his head in sarcastic humor. "You're good at scenes, though, aren't you? That was a hell of an interesting one you played out for that dude you've been sleeping with. He bought the whole story, too. But maybe that's because there was a lot of truth in it. I'll bet he really had begun to bore you. After all, we both know your taste in men runs more toward guys like me."

"Eleven years ago I had lamentably poor taste in men."

"Better watch that tongue, babe. I'm not in a mood to take any of your sass this evening."

"Yes, I know. You're here to conduct business." Heather concentrated on the coffee she was preparing. "What happens after your partner shows up and the two of you have finished your deal?"

She sensed his unpleasant grin. "You mean what happens to you?"

"Under the circumstances, I think it's a legitimate question." Her fingers shook as she used an old rag to shield them from the hot handle of the coffeepot. But her voice was steady. A man like Rick Monroe would derive a great deal of pleasure out of inducing fear in her.

"Funny you should bring up the subject. I've been thinking about that little matter myself. I started thinking about it when I watched you give that other guy his walking papers. I'm going south after tonight...."

"South?" She poured the coffee with unnatural care.

"Yeah. Mexico, or maybe farther. Maybe Panama. Somewhere I can enjoy myself and my money without having a lot of people asking nosy questions. Maybe, just maybe, if you're real nice to me tonight and if you behave yourself while I'm conducting business, I might think about taking you along. Least for a while."

Heather almost panicked at the leer in his tone. "And if I don't want to go with you?"

"Well, babe, I'm sure you can understand that I'm not in a position to tolerate a lot of witnesses," he began calmly. "If you hadn't gotten rid of that ex-boyfriend, for example, I'd have had to get rid of him myself. Permanently."

Heather's eyes squeezed shut for a fraction of a second in silent relief. The knowledge that Jake was safe steadied her as she sought to deal with her own precarious position.

"Since you're in a mood to get rid of people on a permanent basis, I think my own decision is going to be rather simple. I'll come with you, Rick."

"I figured you would." His gaze mocked her cruelly as he sipped his coffee. "Just like old times, huh?"

"Do you really think so?"

"Well," he allowed smoothly, "there will be one major difference. I'll be the one with the money and I'll be the one you'll have to please. That is, if you want to stay alive and healthy."

"I've always believed in staying alive and healthy," Heather said lightly.

"Then we might get along real well together," he declared with nerve-racking satisfaction. "I always kinda wondered how it would have been between you and me. You ever wonder how it would have been if you hadn't gotten on your high horse that day and told me to get lost?"

"Sometimes." The truth was she'd known at the time that she was lucky to be rid of him, even if it had meant hitchhiking all the way to California on her own.

Rick strolled toward her, surveying her as though he was examining new property. Insolently he stood in front of her, catching her chin in the fingers of his right hand. "We'll have a chance to find out now, won't we?" His mouth came down on hers.

Heather cringed beneath the wet pressure of his mouth. Everything that she disliked and feared in the man was in his kiss. Revulsion welled up in her and she was unable to hide it completely.

Angry at her lack of response, Rick crowded closer. "You can do better than that, babe. Remember you're going to have to keep me happy if you want to stay alive." His lips ground down on hers.

Instinctively Heather tried to retreat and the movement enraged Monroe. He dragged her back against him, forcing her into an intimate contact that sent more panic through her.

"No! Rick wait, please."

"Shut up, babe. Show me how nice you're going to be to me. Show me how you're going to pay your way to Mexico. I always wondered how you'd be in bed. Did you know that? I figured that maybe if a man got control of you instead of being under your thumb he might be able to handle you. I was going to take over once I got my hands on some of your father's cash. But I never got the chance. This time things'll be different. This time everything's going to be on my terms."

My terms. The words rang in Heather's ears. How many times had she said that to Jake? *I'm coming back to Tucson on my terms.* The marriage was to have been on her terms. The Hacienda Strand was to have been run on her terms. As she listened to Rick Monroe make a similar declaration she realized how appallingly arrogant she must have sounded to Jake.

"Rick, please, can't we talk? It's been so long and so much has happened."

"I might as well tell you that I don't like chatty females," he growled. "Never did. And you were always wantin' to go on and on about something. All those years ago I didn't have much choice except to listen. But that's something else that's going to be different now." He lowered his head again.

Heather endured the kiss, sensing that for the moment at least, Rick wasn't going to go any further. He was too tense waiting for his mysterious partner to show up, she decided. She was in no immediate danger of rape. Monroe had other things on his mind, fortunately. She stopped fighting the disgusting embrace and Rick finally lifted his head, looking satisfied.

"That's better. You just remember who's in charge and we'll get along okay, you and me. Okay." He nodded to himself and fingered the handle of the gun again.

It was the way he toyed with the weapon that disturbed her more than anything else. What was he going to do to that partner after the deal had been transacted? Her own fate seemed even more precarious. There was so little chance that, even if he had understood that she was in trouble, Jake would be able to get help and get back up this canyon. The storm was raging more violently than ever outside. The heavy cloud cover coupled with approaching night cast an impenetrable gloom over the entire canyon. Outside, the sound of the swollen stream was becoming louder, turning into a dull roar as it pounded down the mountain.

"I'll remember you're in charge, Rick." Desperately she sought to inject suitable meakness into her tone. It was an effort to force down the instinctive anger and rebellion that threatened to dictate her words. Her natural desire to fight back could easily get her killed.

"Good. Let's have some more of that coffee. And see what you can rustle up for dinner. I'm going to get a lamp from the jeep. We got another hour or so to wait."

"What will you do if your partner can't get up this canyon tonight?" Obediently Heather went into the kitchen area to select some canned goods from the supply she had brought.

"He'll make it." Rick opened the door. "The road's still passable. Believe me, this deal is too big. Joe will be here come hell or—" he paused to snicker over his own joke "—high water." Leaving the door open so that he could keep an eye on Heather, he dashed out to the jeep and grabbed a battery-powered lamp. A moment later he was back, slamming the door behind him as he turned on the portable lamp.

Heather warmed the soup and dug out some crackers. As the minutes ticked past she became increasingly frightened. Rick was concentrating on watching the road to the cabin through the broken window. He seemed more tense than ever.

If she was going to do anything it had better be before the man named Joe arrived. There was no sense in praying for rescue now. She had to accept the possibility that Jake had left earlier without having understood she was in danger. Chewing on her lower lip, Heather eyed the pan of bubbling soup. Perhaps if she hurled the contents at Monroe she could make it through the door before he recovered.

Such an impossible long shot. And he had that gun. He was fiddling with it again, taking it out of his belt and examining it as if to be sure it was in proper working order. Oh, God. A pan of soup against a gun.

First she had to lure him closer to the stove, and somehow she had to get him to stuff the gun back into his belt. So impossible. So hopeless.

That last thought made her grit her teeth silently. The one thing she had always been was a fighter. She'd never lacked spirit even when the odds were heavily against her. With her own life at stake she certainly wasn't going to get weak-kneed now!

"Rick, the soup's ready."

"Bring a bowl of it over here," he ordered negligently. "I want to stay where I can keep an eye on the road."

He was bound to be suspicious if she walked across the room carrying the whole panful of soup instead of just a small bowl. The odds were getting worse by the minute. The only positive note was that he'd stuck the gun in his belt again.

Heather was standing very still, a bowl in one hand, the rag-wrapped handle of the soup pan in the other, when she saw the shadowy movement outside the side window. She barely stifled her gasp of alarm. Perhaps Rick's friend Joe had some plans of his own this evening. He might have been the one she'd seen so briefly moving past the window. Or it might be rescue for her. Or nothing.

Rick was still staring out the broken panes of the front window, unaware of her frozen state. Heather was chilled with fear. If she had seen someone moving past the other window and that someone was Joe she was probably already as good as dead. Drug deals such as the one Rick apparently had going tonight all too often left the bodies of witnesses and former "partners" in their wake.

And then quite suddenly a loud crash echoed through the room. It was followed by the sound of splintering glass and disorienting splashes of light and shadow as the battery-operated lamp went spinning to the floor to land behind the kitchen counter.

Heather cried out as the dark form of a man came hurtling through the side window. In the shadows it was impossible to see his face. Rick spun around, clawing for the gun in his belt.

Before he could get the weapon clear, the intruder had thrown himself against him. Both men fell to the wooden floor with a jolting thud.

8

THE GLARING LIGHT of the battery lamp glowed bravely from its overturned position, but the only object in the room clearly illuminated by it was Heather's stricken face. The far end of the room near the door was in almost total darkness as the two men on the floor fought savagely.

It took an instant for Heather to break the bonds of her own shock and then she was galvanized into action. Whatever chance she was going to have was here and now. The man who had come in through the window in such a dramatic fashion must be the mysterious Joe. He'd probably arrived in such a manner in an effort to rid himself of a no longer useful partner, Heather decided.

Dropping the bowl and the pan of soup she started to run for the door. Instinct made her hesitate, turn back and yank open one of the kitchen drawers she had searched earlier. She thought she had seen a flashlight inside.

It was there, although heaven only knew if it had any working batteries in it. There was no time to experiment. Whirling again she dashed for the door.

The fierce struggle on the floor spilled over into her path, forcing her to detour around the dark heaving shapes of the men. It seemed to her the battle was being fought in an unnatural silence.

No cries or shouts or screams of protest or anger sounded in the small heavily shadowed room, only sickening thuds and blows and muffled gasps. Somehow the very lack of human yelling only served to emphasize the viciousness of the conflict.

Heather frantically danced around the unpredictable flow of battle, dodging first a foot and then an arm that was flung into her path. Breathing heavily, her pulse pounding, she grabbed the door handle and yanked.

Outside the rain was coming down as violently as the fight behind her was raging. The storm had turned into a nightmare of roaring water and darkness. Driving would be almost impossible now, even if she could get the Mercedes around the jeep that Rick had parked behind it.

Fumbling with the flashlight, Heather was relieved to find it still produced a weak beam. It must have been a light that Rick had left behind during one of his periodic "business" trips up to the cabin, she reasoned.

She was standing on the porch poised for flight, trying to find the Mercedes keys in her pocket when, with muffled groans, the two men locked in savage combat burst through the doorway.

Heather's startled scream was broken off abruptly as she dashed out of the way. Her pale flashlight beam swung jaggedly across the two figures as they tumbled past her and down the short flight of steps into the mud. The driving rain pummeled both as they were seemingly half absorbed by the elements.

It was as the beam of light darted haphazardly across a booted foot that Heather caught her breath. She recognized the low-cut desert boot even as it nearly tripped her.

"Jake!"

He didn't answer, of course. He probably didn't even hear her. Jake had his hands full from what Heather could see, as he tried to avoid being the one on the bottom while the two men struggled for supremacy in the mud.

"Oh, my God, *Jake!*"

He had come for her. He had gotten her message; understood that she needed him and he had returned to rescue her.

That thought pounded through Heather's head, nearly swamping the more practical considerations of the moment. The man she loved had returned to her side when she needed him.

The mud at the bottom of the steps seemed to be absorbing some of the violence. The blows the two men delivered required more and more effort. They were both tiring and the violence of the elements hindered the efforts each was making.

Frantically Heather tried to find a loose board or a piece of kindling wood, anything to use against Rick Monroe. Then it occurred to her that in the darkness, with only the aid of the weak flashlight, she would have a tough time determining which man was Rick at any given second. From what she could see both were thoroughly coated in muddy sand and grit.

Even as she was trying to decide how to assist Jake one of the rain-darkened figures emerged from the tangle of violence. Heather's flashlight caught a frightening silhouette as the man on top briefly straddled the one on the ground, then raised an arm for a final blow.

It landed an instant later with a sickening sound, and then there was sudden stillness. Heather swung the light in her hand to the face of the man who was slowly struggling to his feet.

"Jake?" she whispered tremulously.

"I swear, Heather, if you intend to give me this kind of trouble for the next fifty years I'm going to resort to beating you regularly on Saturday nights whether you need it or not."

"Oh, Jake!" She whipped down the steps, hurling herself against his mud-splattered figure. The rain pelted them heavily but Heather was aware of nothing except the feel of Jake's strong arms as they came around her. "Oh, Jake, I was so afraid. I couldn't see who it was coming in through the window and I thought it might be Rick's partner."

"His partner? You mean there's more than one of these guys hanging around?"

"There's an old saying that snakes travel in pairs. Jake, you're hurt." Anxiously Heather tried to step free of him, her fingers going to the trail of red her flashlight picked out on the side of his face.

"You can say that again," he agreed feelingly. "I hurt all over. By tomorrow I'm going to be black and blue. Tell me about this partner."

"Someone named Joe is supposed to rendezvous with Rick tonight. They have a deal going. Drugs, I think. He's due any minute, that is if the road hasn't become totally impassable."

"Oh, hell. That's just wonderful," Jake growled in disgust. "You never do anything halfway, do you?"

"Jake, this is hardly my fault!"

"We'll discuss that matter in more detail at a later date. Have you got the keys to the Mercedes?"

The urgent command in him silenced further protest. Mutely Heather handed him the keys. Then he caught her wrist and yanked her toward the car.

"I'm not sure if we'll be able to drive out of this canyon. We'll go as far as we can and then walk the rest of the way if necessary," he told her as he opened the front door of the car.

"Walk? Jake, it's miles back to Tucson. It would take forever to walk."

"We may not have much option."

He glanced skyward as another roll of thunder crashed above them. Then a beam of light flashed around the curve of the road. An instant later the sound of a jeep engine cut through the endless roar of the rain.

Heather caught her breath as she glanced back down the winding road. "Joe," she whispered. "That must be Rick's partner, Joe."

"And if he's anything like your old pal, Rick, he'll be armed. That really tears it. Come on, Heather. We'll never get this car turned around and headed down that road before that jeep gets here."

"But where are we going?" she protested as he pulled her away from the car and back toward Rick's crumpled figure.

"First we'll try to even the score. Your friend Rick here had a gun...."

"Will you stop calling him my friend? The guy was going to kidnap me. Possibly kill me. He didn't want any witnesses to his little deal with Joe!"

"Not my fault you cultivate weird friends," Jake retorted sardonically as he flipped Monroe's unconscious body over. "I can hardly see a thing. Hand me that flashlight."

Stifling an urge to defend herself, Heather obeyed. As she watched Jake swiftly search Monroe's muddy figure it occurred to her that she was seeing a side of her lover she would never have guessed existed two days ago. He had fought Rick with an efficient savagery that implied it wasn't the first time he'd found himself in a muddy brawl. And now he went looking for a gun as if he'd know how to use it when he found it. Heather shivered as she tried to watch him through the rain.

"Damn. He must have lost it while we were rolling around down here in the mud. Even if I could find it, there's no telling what kind of condition it would be in now." Behind Jake the jeep's engine grew louder. "Let's go. If we stay here we're going to be sitting ducks in the beam of those headlights." He switched off the weak flashlight in his hand just as the jeep rounded the last turn in the road.

"Why did you turn it off? I can't see a thing."

"The flashlight pinpointed us in the darkness. Come on, Heather, quit dragging your feet."

"Dragging my feet! I'm hardly able to move in this mud. The driveway's turning into a river. Where are we going?"

"Back behind the cabin. There's no way out for us down that road." Jake tugged her after him, forcing her to run blindly in the pelting rain. She realized vaguely that they were circling the cabin, putting the structure between themselves and whoever was in the jeep.

The engine noise was cut abruptly and Heather knew Rick's partner was in the driveway.

"In another couple of seconds he'll realize that's Monroe lying unconscious in the mud. Unfortunately, I'm not sure how long Monroe will stay unconscious. I should have hit him harder." Jake sounded as if he was berating himself.

"Jake, we can't go much farther in this direction. The canyon walls become very steep back here and we'll never be able to climb them in this rain. I wouldn't be surprised if there have already been some mud slides."

"There's not much cover around here, either, from what I could tell earlier when I was working my way around the place to get to you." Jake swore with soft violence. "We'll have to ford that stream. Once we're on the far side we'll have more cover and we can make our way back down out of the canyon."

"That little stream is a river by now. I can hear it roaring past us. Jake, we'll never make it across."

A shot rang out in the darkness and Jake reacted by shoving Heather violently forward. "Move, woman," he hissed. "Good old Joe obviously knows he's not alone out here."

Stumbling along, unable to see more than the fleeting outlines of shadows through the pouring rain and enveloping darkness, Heather obeyed. Jake never released her hand as they floundered farther back into the depths of the canyon. Behind them another shot split the night.

"He's aiming wildly. Can't see anything more than we can at the moment. Just trying to scare us. For all he knows we're armed too."

"He can't even know if there's more than one of us," Heather offered hopefully.

"Unless Monroe wakes up and tells him."

"You think that's likely?"

"He was coming around while I was searching for the gun. Yeah, it's likely. We'll have to assume there's two of them looking for us and we'll also have to assume they're both armed. Even if Monroe can't find his own gun, his pal Joe may have brought more than one."

A beam of light arced through the night, slicing over their heads. Jake froze, holding Heather absolutely still.

"What was that?" she whispered, leaning heavily against his side.

"They've got a light, obviously. A strong one and it must be portable. Probably use it for hunting at night."

"Deer hunting?"

"I have a hunch the only game those two find challenging is the two-footed kind. Keep your head down. We're going to have to get across that stream."

Heather wanted to protest again. She'd lived in this area a lot longer than Jake had and she knew how treacherous the canyon streams could become in this kind of storm. But she had no better plan to offer. From what she remembered of the terrain she knew they would soon be out of running room. Farther into the canyon the going would be impossible and the stream itself would be more confined and therefore more violent as it surged between the rocky walls.

Another shot cut the sounds of the storm, and the powerful beam of the hunting light flashed alongside, barely missing them. And then she heard Rick's voice calling out.

"Heather, come back here. You'll be okay. You know that. I told you I'd take you with me to Mexico. You can't get out of this canyon. Leave that joker and come back to the cabin. I'll take care of you."

"I knew I should have hit him again," Jake gritted.

"Jake, this is about as far as we can go," Heather gasped as the hunting light cut across the canyon walls in front of her. She used it to get her bearings. "Much farther and there won't be any chance at all of getting across the stream. It will be pouring through that upper canyon like a runaway train by now. I'm not even sure we can make it across here." The arcing light swept off to her right.

"They're focusing the searchlight on this side of the canyon," Jake muttered, watching the sweep of light. "They obviously don't expect us to try the stream."

"Rick knows this area. He'll assume we'll have more sense than to try crossing a flooding mountain stream in weather like this."

"You're sure?"

"I'm sure. Anyone who's ever lived for any length of time in the desert knows better than to get in the middle of a dry wash or a mountain stream when the thunderstorms hit like this."

"Then we really don't have a choice. We'll have to risk it. They'll be concentrating their search on the right-hand side of the canyon."

"Logically, yes."

Carefully Jake edged toward the left, feeling his way. He kept his fingers lashed tightly around Heather's wrist. The usually murmuring stream was in full roar, well over its banks and rising quickly. It tumbled down its path out of the canyon with an energy that was awesome. In the darkness Heather couldn't see the far side.

"Jake, we'll never make it," she said flatly as her foot sank into the slippery sand on the stream's edge.

"We haven't got much choice." He released her momentarily to fumble at his waist.

"What are you doing?"

"I'm going to chain us together. Hand me your belt."

Another shot cracked through the darkness but the light was definitely playing on the canyon wall, not on the stream.

"It won't be long before Rick realizes we must have tried the stream after all," Heather offered, trying to keep her voice even. This was no time to allow the fear she was feeling to show. Plenty of time to break down and have a fit of hysterics later, she assured herself bracingly.

"Then we'd better get moving." Stepping close to Heather, Jake fed the end of her belt through three of the belt loops on the side of her jeans. Then he threaded his own belt through three of the loops on his own jeans. Heather peered down, watching intently as he then intertwined both lengths of leather and fastened each belt to create a chain of leather a couple feet long stretching between them.

"It'll hold as long as the belt loops hold," Jake rasped. "All right, let's go."

He circled her wrist once more in a grip of iron and plunged into the raging stream. Heather stumbled in behind him and nearly lost her breath as the impact of the water struck her. Even Jake's strong body gave beneath the force of the water. They both scrambled for footing and found it only after being carried a few feet downstream. Jake pulled himself upright, tugging Heather up beside him. She gasped for air.

Fortunately, although the water was flowing furiously, it was only about waist high at this point. Underfoot Heather felt the slipping sliding surfaces of rocks that were being pushed along the bottom of the streambed. It made it impossible to keep one's footing for more than a few seconds at a time.

Only the vague outline of boulders on the far side guided them. Jake struck out for the uncertain safety with all the single-minded determination Heather had instinctively known he possessed. She was pulled along behind him, frequently feeling the chain of belts go taut.

She estimated that they were probably halfway across when the first of the denim belt loops on her jeans gave way.

"Jake!"

"Hang on," he growled above the roar of the water. His fingers tightened even more forcefully around her wrist.

If Rick and his pal Joe were still firing wildly into the darkness, Heather could no longer hear the shots above the flooding waters. The only important thing in the world right now was getting to the tentative safety of the boulders on the far side of the stream. As she stumbled and fell again and again, she occasionally caught sight of the shadowy rocky outline. Jake's strong grasp was the only other point of reference in an environment gone mad.

A stronger surge of water crashed into them and under the force of it Jake was shoved sideways. His grip on Heather's wrist slackened momentarily and then broke. Only the belts held the two floundering people together during the desperate seconds it took for Jake to reclaim his footing and Heather's wrist.

In those few seconds of heightened strain, Heather felt the second belt loop give way. The fabric of the fancy designer jeans simply wasn't going to survive the strain being placed upon it.

The force of the water was increasing by the minute. Every step Heather took seemed to be much harder than the last. By the time she thought they might be three-quarters of the way across, the last belt loop gave way.

"Here, hold onto the end of the belt with your free hand. It's not much but it's something. Loop it around your wrist," Jake shouted over the thundering water.

Heather obeyed. Hanging on to the end of the belt with one hand and clasping Jake's fingers with the other, she salvaged what energy was left for breathing. Every time she was knocked down in the water the task of gasping for air got much harder.

The sound of the raging waters seemed to escalate. The tightly confined waters in the upper canyon were surging powerfully as the rains increased. Heather clenched her teeth and fought for the next step. She knew that neither she nor Jake could battle much farther in this fashion.

And then she sensed a slight rise in the streambed. Another few feet and they would be on the far side. But the roar of approaching water was deafening as tons of it came cascading down the canyon.

She felt Jake come to a halt. Her own body was sent crashing into his as he braced himself in what was still waist-high water. His hands were suddenly under her arms, lifting her up toward the boulders that promised safety.

Desperately Heather grasped, pulling herself up along the wet slippery surface. Her scrabbling shoes found purchase for a moment and then she was almost free of the pull of the water.

The leather belt that she had been hanging on to for dear life started to slip through her fingers.

"Jake," she cried, realizing what was happening. She grabbed for the end of the belt with both hands and, lying flat on the surface of the rock, held tight.

"Let go, Heather. You'll only get pulled back into the water," he yelled.

She knew what was going to happen. She had made it up out of the waters and onto the relative safety of the rocks because she'd had someone to lift her up and out. There was no one behind Jake to provide that impetus. If she couldn't pull him out, he would never make it. The force of the water was simply too powerful.

"I'm going to pull you out, Jake!" she shouted.

"You can't. You're not strong enough. Let go of the belt, damn it!" It was an order, delivered with all the force of a man who meant to be obeyed.

Heather ignored it, wriggling backward along the rock until she was over a small ridge in the boulder. Angling the leather strap over the ridge, she looped it around her wrist and tugged with every ounce of her being.

"Heather! Let go!"

She didn't bother to answer. It was a totally ridiculous suggestion; anyhow, there was literally no way she could release the belt unless it tore off her hand. Releasing it would be to give Jake over to the hurtling waters. Impossible.

Arms stretched overhead, feeling as though they were about to be torn from their sockets, Heather used the ridge of the rock as a fulcrum for the leather. It provided a hard edge that would not give way. As long as she could hold on to the end of the belt and as long as the loops on Jake's jeans did not give way she could hold on to the man she loved.

With an intense grimness she began inching down the far side of the rock. The trip was made in increments of centimeters but it was slowly, painfully being accomplished. Apparently Jake had stopped trying to fight her and was assisting in his own rescue effort.

Time became meaningless. All that mattered to Heather was gaining one more fraction of an inch. The leather strap bit into her wrist, the pain intense, but she ignored it. The weight of her body along with the pivot edge provided by the rock combined to give her the vital margin she needed.

The rock curved sharply beneath her and Heather tried to throw herself down the far side, utilizing the full weight of her body to drag the leather a full three inches.

Abruptly the bite of the leather around her wrist slackened. Heather jerked her head up, aware that something had given way. Either Jake had found a way to free himself and was being carried helplessly downstream or . . .

"Lady, one of these days I'm going to teach you how to obey simple straightforward orders, if it's the last thing I do on earth."

Heather looked up, stunned, to find him staring down at her from the top of the rock.

"But not today," he concluded as he scrambled over the rise of the boulder and dropped down beside her. "Not today." He reached for her with a husky sound.

And then she was in his arms, clinging madly. The rain continued to drench them but they were clear of the raging waters of the stream and out of reach of the two men who were hunting them.

"There's no way anyone else is going to get across that flood tonight," Jake said into her streaming wet hair, echoing her thoughts. "We're safe for now. My God, woman, you've scared the living daylights out of me one too many times today. It's going to take me weeks to recover."

Her face buried in his soaking-wet shirt, Heather shook her head in a fierce little negative movement. "Something tells me you handle days like this quite well. Jake Cavender, you're a fraud. How did you manage to deceive my sweet unsuspecting parents into thinking you were a nice guy who also happened to be a financial wizard when it came to hotels?"

His arms tightened around her. "There was no deception involved," he assured her thickly. "I am a nice guy. And I am good at accounting and business planning. It's just that when I'm around you, I find myself acting out of character." He pulled back a bit, framing her face in his hands. "Heather, you saved my life a few minutes ago."

She looked up at him, smiling mistily through the rain that was pelting her face. "You saved me back there at the cabin. As everyone keeps saying, I guess we make a good team."

In the wet darkness she could barely distinguish the gleaming depths of his eyes as he gazed down at her intently.

"Remember that." Then he turned, catching her wrist one more time. "Come on, honey. We can't stay here. This rain is going to go on forever. We need to find some kind of shelter."

"Ouch! Jake, my wrist. Let go of my wrist!"

"What the . . . ?" He released her instantly. "What happened?"

"Nothing," she said quickly, gently touching the raw burn that circled the base of her hand. "It's just that I had the belt looped around my wrist."

"And it hurts like hell where the leather cut into your skin," he acknowledged grimly. Gently he took her other hand instead, and together they forged an awkward path through the rain-soaked night.

"There used to be a couple of old deserted cabins on this side of the stream," Heather said hesitantly, trying to pick out familiar landmarks in the shadows. "One I remember was about a mile downstream from ours."

"A mile in this country is going to take some doing. But I guess it's our best bet."

"I'm not really sure it's going to be safe to stay there. It was fairly close to the stream, as I recall, and the way that water is rising it will inundate everything in its path. I wouldn't be surprised if Dad's old cabin is gone by morning. This torrent is going to do some real damage before the night's over."

"Then we'd better keep moving until we can get well out of the path of that water."

He was right, Heather knew, but she wasn't at all sure she was going to have the strength to hike any great distance. Fording the flooding stream and pulling Jake out of the water had sapped an incredible amount of energy. But she decided not to bring up the subject of her own weariness. There was no point because they had no choice but to keep going.

"I wonder what Rick and his friend are doing," she remarked a few minutes later.

"They've probably given up the search by now. I can still see a light way over there on the far shore so I suppose they're still at the cabin. Don't worry, though, there's no way they can get to us," Jake said reassuringly.

"That water's going to be over the road if it isn't already. They'll be stranded at that cabin. And if it goes—"

"No loss," Jake cut in callously. "I have a hunch no one would miss those two. What was all that about a drug deal?"

"I think that's what it was supposed to be. Rick arrived at the cabin shortly after I got there this afternoon. When he climbed out of the jeep he was holding a gun."

Jake growled something violent. "Then what happened?"

"He kept saying how rich he was and how much richer he was going to be before tonight was over. Said he'd been using the cabin for 'business' meetings for the past couple of years. He knew about it from the days when he and I used to ride the motorcycle up to the place. He knew then that Dad hardly ever used it and probably guessed it had been used even less during recent years. He was fairly startled to find me there."

"I'll bet," Jake muttered laconically.

"He wasn't exactly delighted to find me at the cabin," Heather went on doggedly, her breath coming in quick gasps as she struggled through the darkened terrain. "But I think he saw, uh, possibilities in the situation."

"I can guess."

Heather ignored the savage tone of his voice. "But when you showed up he really had no use for you at all. He . . . he threatened to kill you if I didn't get rid of you, Jake."

"So you acted out the big rejection scene? Watch out for that soft sand. I just put a foot in it and it felt almost like quicksand. Keep a little more to the right."

"I didn't have much choice—about the rejection scene," Heather said pleadingly. "It was the only thing I could think of on the spur of the moment."

"You do have a flair for drama."

"That's what Rick said," she admitted miserably. Actually, she was feeling more and more miserable by the moment. Although the desert night was not really cold, she was beginning to feel chilled in her wet clothing. The rain seemed never ending and the dull roar of the stream made her uncomfortably aware of how close it still was. The only source of comfort was Jake's firm grip on her hand.

"Did you think I'd just meekly walk out the door the way I did?" Jake sounded almost curious.

"Well, to tell you the truth, I was hoping you'd figure out that something was drastically wrong. I told myself you might realize that even if I was going to spend a few days with another man, Rick Monroe would hardly be the one I'd choose!"

"What did you expect me to do?"

"Go for help."

"There wouldn't have been time to get down out of this canyon, convince someone you needed help and get back. Not with the way this storm was breaking."

"By the time night had fallen I figured that much out for myself. I was contemplating throwing a pan of hot soup at Rick when you came charging through the window. The only trouble was, I couldn't see who it was coming through that window. I was afraid it might be Rick's partner. Jake, how did you know something was really wrong?"

She thought he turned back briefly to look at her with an expression of amazement, but it was difficult to tell. The amazement was definitely in his voice, however, along with a few other emotions such as scorn, disgust and a not-so-subtle masculine comment on her intelligence.

"I find you blithely declaring you're going to spend a few days with another man within twenty-four hours of having been in my bed, and you wonder how I knew something was wrong?"

Despite the increasing chill of the night air on her damp body, Heather warmed. Her smile wasn't visible in the darkness but Jake probably sensed it.

"Yeah, I thought that might tip you off," she murmured with sweet satisfaction. "But how did you know he had a gun and that the situation was so dangerous?"

"I didn't. I didn't know what the hell was going on. I only figured you wouldn't have the nerve to pull that dramatic milady-dismissing-her-lover scene on me unless there was a lot more going on than appeared on the surface. I decided to drive the car out of sight and then hike back to get a better look at the situation. By then it was growing dark. I saw Monroe go out to get a lamp from his jeep and realized he had a gun. So I decided to wait until it was really dark before trying to take him."

"Which you did very efficiently. Jake, where on earth did you learn to fight like that?" Heather demanded.

"I didn't grow up with your advantages, remember? I had to compensate," he told her dryly. But he gave her hand a warm squeeze. "Where did you learn to hang on in a situation where you should have had sense enough to let go?"

"I was always a little on the stubborn side. Just ask my folks."

"Stubborn and rebellious, and much too headstrong for your own good," Jake agreed softly. "And I owe my life to all those rather unmanageable qualities."

"We're even. I owe you mine."

"A real team, hmm?"

"Yes, Jake."

"Well, teammate, I think I see something that looks as if it could be that cabin you mentioned. The one that was about a mile downstream from your dad's place. Let's give it a try. We need shelter for the rest of the night."

He was right. They were both exhausted and soaked. Not a good combination. To Heather's relief the cabin proved to be on much higher ground than she had remembered. It was nestled into the hillside, well above the threat of flowing water. And when Jake pushed open the unlocked door the single room appeared relatively dry.

"Do you think this place is safe enough? You're more familiar with the dangers of this kind of storm than I am." Jake glanced around assessingly.

"Yes, I think we'll be fine. We should probably keep an eye on the level of the stream during the night. Check it a few times. But this place is higher on the hillside than I remembered. Besides, both this place and my dad's have come through storms like this before. The people who built them must have had a certain amount of respect for the elements or the cabins would have been swept away years ago. One way or another, it doesn't make much difference. I don't think I could go another step."

"You're shaking," Jake muttered, pulling her close to him for a moment. Then he abruptly released her. "I'll see if there's anything we can use to build a fire."

"Even a light would help. I'll look for some candles."

Heather found the candles in a kitchen drawer before Jake discovered the small storage shed on the back porch. But even as she was using the matches that had accompanied the candles in the drawer, he was pushing back through the door with an armload of wood.

"It's fairly dry from what I can tell in the darkness. With any luck we can have a real fire."

"I can't think of anything I want more at the moment," Heather said fervently.

"See if you can turn up any blankets." Jake knelt down in front of the hearth to busy himself with the firewood and the matches. He had a small blaze going by the time Heather located a couple of dusty blankets in a narrow closet.

"They're filthy," she complained.

"Better than nothing. Let's get out of these clothes." He got to his feet, peeling off his wet shirt without any hesitation at all.

His hands were on the fastening of his jeans when Heather's shaking fingers finally started in on her own buttons.

"What's the matter, honey? My God. You're so cold. Come closer to the fire. I'll take care of you. Here, let me undo those buttons."

The warm concern was an invitation she couldn't resist. With a small moan of relief, Heather moved into his arms and turned her face into the bare skin of his chest.

"Oh, Jake, I was so scared," she confided huskily. "I've never been as frightened in my whole life as I was this afternoon."

"You think I wasn't?" he retorted hoarsely. "In between worrying about what kind of trouble you might be in, I worried about whether or not you'd told me the truth, whether or not you were really trying to get rid of me."

"You actually thought I might have wanted to spend a few days with Rick Monroe after spending a night with you? Never, Jake. *Never!*' Convulsively she wrapped her arms around his waist, holding herself close to his comforting strength. "All the while I was telling you to get lost I kept praying you could read my mind."

"And I kept praying you were trying to give me some other message than the verbal one. Not that it would have made a heck of a lot of difference. One way or another I had no intention of letting you spend the night with Monroe. I told you last night that you belong to me."

"Yes, Jake." She nestled against him trustingly as he pushed the damp shirt off her shoulders and then unfastened her jeans.

"I also had a hunch you knew it and that you wouldn't have the courage to throw another man in my face."

"Never."

"Stop shaking, honey," he begged as he slid his palms inside her jeans and peeled them down over her hips. The wet underpanties went with the denim. "You're so cold." His hands moved chafingly on her back.

"Reaction." The single word of explanation came out on a slight stutter.

Jake released her to pick up the blanket and wrap it around her. Then he hurriedly stripped off the remainder of his own clothing. The flickering firelight on his body captivated her. It danced along the solid male flanks and set primitive golden shadows over his chest. She loved him and he was beautiful to her eyes.

"I'll get these cushions over there by the fire. We can use them for a bed," Jake said as he pulled the dusty sofa cushions free and tossed them down in front of the fire.

"A rather narrow bed," Heather observed dubiously.

He looked at her as the last cushion went down in front of the flames. "We'll make do, won't we?"

She nodded wordlessly, unable to meet the searching challenge in his eyes.

"Heather, honey," he muttered, catching her by the shoulders and pulling her close. "You're not still frightened are you? Of me this time?"

"No." But she couldn't find the words to explain exactly what she was feeling, so she tried to make light of it all. "You saved my life. How could I be frightened of you? I told you, I'm shaking a little from the cold and the wet and the reaction."

He dropped to his knees on the sofa cushions and gently tugged her down beside him. When she was kneeling in front of him he tenderly stroked her back beneath the blanket.

"Come and lie down with me," he commanded softly. "And I'll keep you warm and safe tonight."

9

HEATHER DIDN'T HESITATE any longer. Relaxing completely into his warmth, she let Jake push her down onto the cushions and fold the blankets over both of them. The heat of his body as he sprawled heavily along her slenderness was more satisfying than any fire, and the strength of his grasp as he cradled her chased away the last of the night's terrors.

"All afternoon and evening I've been torn between the temptation to beat you for getting yourself into such a stupid mess and the equally strong temptation to do this." Jake's mouth found hers in a deep caress that brought a moan to the back of Heather's throat.

His hand moved along her side, down to her hip and back up to her breasts. The reviving touch was more sensual than therapeutic, although it certainly served to dispel the chills.

"I'd much rather you gave in to this temptation than have you beat me," Heather murmured gently, spearing her fingers through his damp hair.

"Since it was my fault you got into the mess with Monroe, I suppose it really wouldn't be fair to take out my frustrations on your sweet backside."

"Your fault?"

"Sure. I should have known better than to let you head for that cabin this morning. I told myself you needed a little time to adjust to matters after what happened yesterday, but by the time I got back to the Hacienda I realized I'd been a fool. Never let a headstrong female go chasing off on her own to think things over. That's my new motto."

"Why did you change your mind and come after me?"

"I figured that if you really needed to do any adjusting it might as well be where I could keep an eye on you."

"If you want to know the truth, I was rather expecting you to arrive. It didn't surprise me at all when you drove up to the cabin. I was terrified about what Rick might do, but I wasn't surprised to see you."

"Good. I do believe we're making progress." Jake sounded complacent and satisfied. "Hold me, honey. Wrap yourself around me and let me know you're here safe in my arms."

"I think I need the same reassurance. I was so afraid I would lose you in the water, Jake. So scared...."

"It's all right, honey," he soothed huskily as he crowded closer. He began to string tense, barely restrained kisses down her shoulder while slowly moving his thighs against hers.

Heather's love for him washed through her, leaving her swamped with breathless excitement. The feel of his rapidly hardening body made her senses sing. She clung to him as tightly as she had clung to him during the trek across the surging canyon waters, and Jake responded.

"You're not cold anymore," he grated as his teeth closed tantalizingly around one nipple. "I can feel you starting to melt, in fact."

"How could I ever be cold around you?"

She felt so good lying beneath him, Jake thought with savage wonder. It was taking all his will to be tender and slow tonight. After the strain he had been through today his every instinct was to crush her to him and imprint his body on hers.

What a fool he'd been to let her go off on her own. He'd realized his mistake relatively quickly, he supposed, but by then it was too late. She had already landed herself in enough trouble to last a lifetime. When he'd walked into that cabin and seen her with another man he'd nearly lost his head.

"I could have killed him," he ground out against her skin.

"It's over, Jake. It's all over," she crooned, understanding instantly.

"Don't ever do that to me again."

"Leave you? Or get into trouble?" she teased gently, her nails making searing little paths over his back.

"Either."

"I'll try to behave more sedately in future," she promised demurely.

Her deliberate though light mockery was more than he could take at the moment. Forcefully Jake pushed his knee between hers, making her fully aware of his own state of readiness. She responded satisfactorily, catching her breath and making that soft feminine animal sound that he had learned last night fascinated him.

"In the morning you're going to come home with me," he told her between kisses. The soft satin skin of her stomach awed him.

"Yes, Jake."

"No more running off to think things over," he continued. He trailed his palm down to the curve of her hip, delighting in the shape of it.

"No, Jake."

"You and I belong together."

"Yes, Jake."

"I like the way you say that," he growled. "Heather, you make me go crazy, do you know that? Out of my head. I've never met a woman who affects me the way you do. God, you're soft. So soft. Put your legs around me. I love the way you cling to me when you're on fire. As if you'll never let go."

"I won't let go," he heard her murmur into his chest. "Ever."

This time he wouldn't make the mistake of letting her think things over in the morning, he vowed silently. She was his and there was no point giving her any more rope. It was time to draw in the slack and let her feel the strength of the cord with which he held her.

Perhaps it was the aftereffects of the traumatic evening events or perhaps he was always going to feel like this when he made love to Heather. Whatever the reason, Jake knew a throbbing excitement in every region of his body. Never had he been so captivated by a woman. After making her his last night he had known he would never be able to let her go. Memories of Rick Monroe in that cabin with her stormed through his head.

"There won't ever be any other men, Heather."

"No. Oh, Jake, I could never want any other man the way I want you."

He heard the promise on her lips and reacted to it with a surge of satisfaction that sent him driving into her soft welcoming body. She opened for him willingly, letting him know just how much he was wanted and needed. He reveled in the way she drew him even closer, her nails biting deeply into his back as her legs clung to his hips.

If there was glory in the taking, there was undiluted pleasure in the giving, Jake discovered. He was enthralled with the way Heather trembled with passion in his arms. Every nuance of her response fed his own desire. When she tightened beneath him, arching her head back over his arm, he thought he would never know such satisfaction as he did in that moment. And then he reminded himself that he would have unlimited moments such as this in the future. She was his now.

His own cry of release was muffled in her hair. Jake lost himself in the woman he was holding and it was a moment or two before he realized exactly what she was saying over and over again as they came down together from the heights.

"I love you, Jake. I love you, I love you, I love you."

The litany caught at him. "Oh, Heather, Heather go on saying it. Just go on saying it forever."

But the exhaustion and the strain had crept up on her. The relaxation of the aftermath of their lovemaking claimed her completely. Smoothing the damp tangled hair back from her forehead, Jake gazed down at Heather as she drifted peacefully into sleep.

She looked soft and trusting, the vivid awareness of the hazel gaze shielded behind bronzed lashes. In this moment she appeared as gentle as a kitten and about as physically strong. Yet she'd held on to that leather

belt coming out of the stream as though she were some
kind of superwoman.

Jake watched her quiet features and decided that he
was not very familiar with that kind of feminine power
and uncompromising determination. Oh, he'd read the
odd news account of a mother who had gone back into
a flaming house to rescue a child, or the tales of women
who, during wartime, fought alongside their men.

It wasn't that he'd ever doubted that the female of the
species could be every bit as fiercely determined as the
male. It was just that in his whole life Jake had never
met a woman who would have exerted herself that
much on his behalf.

Usually women were rather anxious to be rid of him.
Everyone from his mother through that string of foster
mothers had made it clear he was not a particularly
lovable person. The women he had known as lovers,
including his ex-wife, had found him interesting for a
while, at least in bed, but somehow the relationships
had progressed little beyond that point.

The complaints from ex-lovers often centered around
the fact that he worked too hard and that his conversation tended to be limited to the subject of hotels and
the hotel business. The few short-term relationships in
which he'd become involved tended to disintegrate
rapidly when sex and the subject of hotel finances were
no longer enough to hold them together. Jake was rarely
able to tell whether it was the women who began to
withdraw first or he. He'd decided he was fated to go
through life with only fleeting contacts and no sense of
permanency.

Then he had accepted the position of financial con-
sultant to Paul Strand and his life had undergone a ma-

jor change. Paul, unlike other people he had assisted, was genuinely grateful for his expertise, rather than resentful of it. Neither Paul nor Ruth ever grew tired of conversation that centered on the hotel-resort industry, and his own growing interest in the future of the Hacienda Strand had endeared him to the Strands.

When the discussion had turned to the long-term future of the Hacienda, Heather's name had come up with increasing frequency. Paul's decision to retire had also been made known. Jake had been aware he was being gently manipulated but it was in a direction he realized he wanted to go. When Heather had proven amenable everything seemed to be falling neatly into place.

He and Heather really were going to be partners. Jake reluctantly eased himself away from her deliciously limp body, adjusted the dusty blankets around her and got to his feet.

Naked, he spent a few minutes arranging the wet clothing in front of the fire and then he stepped out into the night to try to gauge the flow of the pounding stream. It seemed to him that the rain was lessening and the canyon waters didn't appear to be climbing. He'd set his mental clock to check it again in an hour or so.

Then he walked back into the cabin and slid gratefully down onto the cushions. With deep satisfaction he pulled his partner into his arms and allowed himself to doze.

HEATHER WOKE the next morning with the sense of something having changed in her environment. It took her a moment before she realized the rain was still coming down, although not in such heavy quantities. It wasn't the weather that had changed, then. She opened her eyes and noted that the fire had died out during the night. But that wasn't what seemed different, either.

When she became aware of Jake's heavy leg tangled with hers she knew why she had a sense of everything being different this morning. She and Jake were together and in love.

"Good morning."

His lazy, sleep-thickened greeting made Heather stir and turn languidly in his arms until she lay facing him on the narrow makeshift bed.

"Good morning," she whispered throatily, surveying him with contentment. "Did I remember to tell you last night that I loved you?" her eyes reflected her happiness.

Jake's mouth twisted in his familiar half smile. "You did. But feel free to keep saying it. I like to hear it." He stroked her bare shoulder with his palm.

"I love you, Jake."

He stared at her for a long searching moment and then without a word, leaned over to kiss her softened mouth. She responded happily, her face glowing as he raised his head again. She waited for the answering declaration of love.

"Heather, I want you to know that I'll always take care of you. I'll make sure you have everything you ever need and I'll protect you. You'll have no cause to regret marrying me, honey."

She laughed warmly up at him, twining her arms around his neck. Her eyes gleamed. "I only hope you'll never have cause to regret marrying me. But I must warn you that people have occasionally complained about my behavior in the past."

"But no one's had occasion to see what a really terrific wife you're going to be," he pointed out, turning onto his back so that she lay across his chest.

"True. No doubt I have undiscovered talents in that field."

"No doubt." Jake twisted his hands into her tousled hair and pulled her close for another brief hard kiss.

"Jake, are you very happy?" she demanded whimsically.

"I have never been so content in my life. Yes, I'm happy." He took the question a little more seriously than she had expected—as if he had to stop and think about it.

"You really think we can manage the Hacienda together?" she persisted.

"Yes. I think, as you pointed out, there'll be some trying moments," he added dryly, "but I think we can deal with them."

"I feel quite positive about that approach myself this morning," she said grinning.

"You think you're going to be able to get your own way by dragging me off to bed whenever you can't talk me into something?"

"I'll have fun trying."

"Umm. So will I." Jake hesitated. "We really do have everything going for us, don't we?"

"A perfect situation," she agreed complacently.

"Mutual interests, a combined career, the approval of your family, physical attraction and the ability to function as a team."

"And I love you."

"I'm glad, Heather. That makes it quite perfect, doesn't it?" he asked lightly.

Heather blinked, a sudden wariness marring her happiness. "Not quite."

Jake looked at her strangely, his hands moving in her hair. "What do you mean, not quite?"

"This—" she informed him, leaning down to nip his shoulder teasingly "—is the point where you're supposed to tell me that you love me. Honestly, Jake. For a supposedly brilliant businessman, you're a little slow on the uptake sometimes."

"I've had a rough time of it lately," he murmured by way of apology.

But the wariness in her was flaring higher. Heather refused to respond to the lightness in his tone. "Jake?"

"Hmm?" He was toying with the curve of her breast where it lay pillowed against his chest.

"Jake, you do still want to marry me, don't you?"

"Oh, yes, honey. I still want to marry you."

"Jake," she tried again, a cold fear putting the chill on her warm pleasure this morning. "Jake, you're not just marrying me for all those reasons you listed a minute ago, are you? Do you love me?"

His hands in her hair ceased their rhythmic movement. The gray eyes met hers with clear intent. "Those reasons I listed are all excellent ones for getting married, Heather. We've been telling each other that for a month."

"But do you love me?" she persisted, a raw pain uncurling in the pit of her stomach as she sensed the answer.

"Heather, I've told you I'll give you everything I can. I'll take care of you."

"All I want right now is for you to be honest with me. *Do you love me?*"

He sighed heavily, holding her head with his hands. "Heather, what you and I have going for us is a lot more real, a lot more important than love."

She sucked in her breath. "You don't love me."

Jake's expression darkened. "I want you, I need you and I'll take care of you."

"But you don't love me, do you?" she cried, belatedly trying to push herself away as the shock of his answer hit home.

Jake caught her shoulders, holding her against him and his startlingly grim gaze burned into hers. "How do you define love, Heather?"

"It's what I feel for you," she rasped.

"Really? You're talking to the man you left standing on the chapel steps with a couple hundred wedding guests and your parents to face alone. Remember?"

"Jake, I didn't mean . . . I mean, that has nothing to do with how I feel. . . ." The words tumbled over each other in awkward fashion as she tried to explain.

"You expect me to believe that a woman in love would pull that scene with the motorcycle?" Jake asked too politely.

Heather shook her head frantically. "I didn't know then. All I could think about was finding out that I'd been tricked. I was furious. I felt betrayed. I wanted everyone to know they couldn't get away with treating me as though I was a stupid female who could be manipulated."

"You were passionately angry. Determined to tell me to go to hell."

"Well, yes, but I had a right to be furious."

"Perhaps."

She stared at him uncomprehendingly. "If you understand, then why are you pushing me like this?"

"You had a right to be angry to a certain extent, although I wasn't doing anything to you that you hadn't intended to do to me. I have no doubt you were feeling a lot of intense emotions that morning. But don't expect me to believe that any of those emotions had anything to do with loving me."

"I didn't know I was in love with you then! I didn't realize it until later," she protested.

"After I'd taken you to bed and dragged a surrender out of you. After I'd shown you how good we are together."

"That had nothing to do with it," she cried, and then felt a wave of confusion. Because it had been the next morning that she had realized the extent of her feelings for Jake Cavender. He saw the unwilling realization in her eyes.

"Sweetheart, don't be so hard on yourself," he placated. "You're a creature of passion and spirit. You always do things with flair and a bit of drama. It's natural that after giving yourself to me as completely as you have that you'd tell yourself you must be head over heels in love."

"It's true!"

"After only forty-eight hours? Honey, you don't realize what you're saying. You're reacting to the trauma of the past couple of days. After all, we've been through quite a lot together. We've discovered we're an explosive combination in bed and we've saved each other's lives. For someone with your basically passionate nature that kind of emotional excitement is bound to be translated into a feeling with a powerful label like love."

She shook her head in horrified understanding. "And you don't believe in love, do you?"

"I believe in all the things we have going for us. And I believe in your charming passion. And if you want to tell me and yourself that you're in love I'm certainly not going to complain. I like hearing the words."

"But you can't return them, is that it?"

"Heather, what I feel for you isn't some vague indefinable emotion like love. It's not ephemeral and fleeting or something that will blow hot and cold depending on circumstances and my mood. What I feel is solid and real and based on solid, real, definable factors."

"I'm not a balance sheet, for heaven's sake! Are you saying you find me attractive because everything adds up?"

"Honey, you're getting emotional again," he pointed out gently. "Why don't you save all that heat and fire for our lovemaking when we can both enjoy it?"

"Don't you dare speak to me in that patronizing tone of voice!"

"I'm sorry. I honestly don't mean to upset you," he began gently.

"Well, I am upset. I'm furious. I'm hurt and I'm mad and I'm thoroughly disgusted. Let me go, Jake."

She pushed at his shoulders and he released her, concern on his face as he watched her grope for her damp clothing. He propped himself up on his elbow.

"Heather," he began rather sternly, "this really isn't the time to indulge in one of your passionate little scenes. We've got a long walk ahead of us and we're both going to need our energy. We're also going to have to cooperate."

"Don't worry," she gritted as she yanked on the stiff denim jeans. "I'm feeling very cooperative on the subject of getting out of here."

He eyed her warily. "Are we going to go through this kind of thing every time you don't get your own way? Haven't you grown up at all during the past decade?"

She flung on her shirt and glared down at him. "Oh, yes, Jake. I've grown up during the past ten years. I think I'm at the height of my maturity, as a matter of fact." In her haste to button the shirt, she began on the wrong buttonhole and had to undo everything. The miscalculation infuriated her further. "For the first eighteen years of my life I let my passionate side rule my actions. For the next eleven years I learned to keep that side under control. I ran my life with the realistic, rational, intellectual side of myself. But thanks to you and the events of the past few days both sides are free."

"I can't wait to see the result," he remarked lightly, still trying to coax her out of her mood with teasing humor.

Heather flung up her head as she shoved the ends of her shirt into her jeans. "Oh, you will, Jake. Don't worry about that."

"Does this mean you don't love me anymore?" he asked wistfully.

"You still think this is some little scene that will blow over, don't you?" She reached for her shoes.

"Dealing with you is like dealing with a keg of dynamite." Jake sat up, throwing back the blankets. "Interesting but uncertain."

Heather looked away as he got unself-consciously to his feet and began sorting out his clothing. She was violently aware he was watching her every movement. The knowledge made her feel dismayingly awkward.

"No, Jake. I'm not like a keg of dynamite. You're going to know exactly where you stand with me. No surprises."

He raised a heavy brow. "Meaning?"

"Meaning that I will be quite happy to set it all out in black and white for you." She straightened from tying her left shoe and stood facing him with her hands planted on her hips, fingers splayed wide.

"I think maybe we ought to wait until you've had a chance to calm down," he suggested.

"Why wait? Nothing's going to change as far as I'm concerned."

"No? Aren't you about to withdraw your declaration of undying love?" he challenged, voice hardening for the first time. Methodically he fastened the opening of his jeans. As if the project took great attention, he focused on it, not on her.

"No."

That brought his head up sharply, gray eyes coolly narrowed. "No?"

She watched him from proud unflinching eyes. "No. I love you, Jake...."

"Well, in that case I don't see what all the fuss is about."

"You will."

He dropped his hands from the front of the jeans and waited, looking resigned. "Okay, let's hear the rest of the story."

"I love you and nothing will change that. Not now. I also love the Hacienda and this land." She waved a hand to encompass the high desert valley on which

Tucson had been built, as well as the treacherous canyon where they had spent the night. "I agree that we have a lot in common businesswise and we both seem to want a home. I agree, in fact, with all the intellectual and realistic reasons why we belong together. I'm even willing to acknowledge that we might just possibly be able to work together, even if you do own the hotel."

Relief flashed into the gray eyes. "Then what is this all about?"

"Simple. The other side of me, the side you say is dramatic, passionate and given to scenes, won't be satisfied with a marriage based purely on lots of nice rational reasons. I won't marry for anything less than love."

Jake's eyes closed in brief disgusted dismay. "You just said you were in love."

"I'm not willing to marry until you're capable of loving me," she declared violently.

"Heather, you're not making any sense. You know damn well I can toss you back down on those cushions and make love to you until you cry out for mercy."

Heather swallowed with a trace of nervousness. Jake was suddenly on the verge of losing his temper and that, she had learned, was not a comfortable state of affairs.

"I won't fight you," she whispered. "I'll give you anything you want. Except marriage."

His mouth thinned. "Anything I want?"

"Anything."

"You don't know what you're saying," he told her flatly.

"Yes, I do. I'll give you everything but a wedding."

He scowled. "You'd move in with me? Take over the responsibilities of helping to run the Hacienda? Entertain our business friends just as though you were my wife? Sleep with me? Eat with me? Shower with me? Work with me?"

"Yes," she agreed simply.

Jake's scowl turned into a full-fledged glare. "You're crazy. It would never work."

She shrugged. "I don't see why not?"

He moved his hand in an angry arc. "Heather, your parents are expecting a wedding. Those two hundred-plus guests you left me stranded with the other day will expect a wedding. Your sisters will expect it. The entire staff of the Hacienda will expect it. No one is going to understand or approve of you carrying on a full-scale affair with me, damn it!"

Heather lifted her chin. "I've been known to disappoint people in the past. No one should be terribly surprised if I do it again."

"I won't allow it," he raged tightly.

"You need me. You can't run that hotel successfully without me and you know it!" she challenged.

"You're being totally irrational about this!" Jake blazed.

"Take it or leave it. It's my final offer."

"You're not in a bargaining position, lady."

"You can't force me to the altar."

"What the hell do you expect to accomplish?" He ran his fingers impatiently through his dark hair.

"I'm going to convince you that I love you and I'm going to teach you to learn to love me. I think that's the whole problem, Jake," she went on with intuitive certainty. "I don't think it's my emotional development that's been stymied. It just took a while for both sides of my nature to join properly. You're the one who missed something along the way. I know what love is because I grew up surrounded by it. Even when I was in full rebellion against my father I never doubted that he loved me or that my parents knew what love was. They've always been in love. I grew up with plenty of examples of the emotion so I can recognize it in myself. But you didn't have all those examples, did you?"

"Growing up in a series of foster homes was an excellent example of just how unreliable love can be," he shot back savagely. "Do you have any idea how often someone has told me she loves me? My mother told me that. All those women who ran the homes used to tell me that, and so did the woman I married. Since then I've heard those words from a few other women. I'm willing to bet they all meant it at the time, but whatever emotion they were experiencing sure didn't last long."

"You liked hearing the words from me. You said so!"

"Of course I like hearing them. They're very pleasant to listen to. Especially from you when I've just made you surrender completely," he stormed. "But no one but a fool would trust them. I prefer to put my trust in other kinds of bonds. Those other bonds exist between us, Heather. They form the real basis on which a marriage between us can work."

"Before I realized I love you, I thought they could too. But now I've changed my mind. We can have a terrific working relationship based on those bonds. We can even have an affair based on them. But I will not allow them to be the basis of any marriage between you and me. I won't settle for anything less than love."

"You want words? What's to prevent me from just saying them?" he charged.

"You won't. Not unless you mean them."

"What makes you so sure? I've misled you before."

"I think you'll be very careful how you use the words 'I love you,'" Heather said quietly. "I think you've heard them issued too often. I'm hoping that it will be a matter of pride with you not to use them to lie to me."

"Pride is the key factor here, I think," Jake pounced, stepping forward and catching hold of her. "Your pride is riding high because I didn't return your passionate little declaration of love this morning."

"I'm too proud to marry you for any other reason than love, if that's what you mean," she agreed boldly. "If we're to have this great working partnership going between us it will have to be based on honesty. I'm being totally honest and I expect the same from you. Will you promise me that much, at least, in return?"

"Yes," he replied shortly.

She smiled very brilliantly. "That's a start, I suppose. We'll take it from there. Don't worry, Jake. It won't be so bad. I think you already are half in love with me. I have great hopes for the future."

He stared at her in bewilderment. "You think it's going to be a nice simple evolutionary process? That I'm going to wake up one morning and realize I'm deeply in love?"

"Why not? That's the way it happened to me."

He ignored that. "And in the meantime you're prepared to give me everything I want?"

"People in love tend to be generous," she assured him kindly.

"The hell they are," he growled softly. "You're not being generous at all. You're willing to make the offer because you know I can't accept."

Heather's assurance faltered. "Can't accept?"

"I have a reputation to consider, even if you don't. I refuse to risk offending your parents by having you move in with me. They would never understand that the whole idea was yours and not mine!"

"Oh, that. Don't worry about my parents. They're accustomed to my unpredictable behavior."

"Not anymore, they're not. I told your father that when I brought you back this time, everything would be under control."

"Ah, I see. Told my parents you'd bring me home in chains, is that it?" Heather mocked gently. "That was very foolish of you, Jake. No one has ever succeeded in managing me. I live my life in my own way. On my own terms." Too late she remembered how arrogant that sounded.

Jake reacted to the challenge with cold assessment. "So you keep saying. But sooner or later everyone meets his or her Waterloo, honey. You're stubborn, willful and constitutionally inclined to rebel against authority, but in me you've met your match. We're not going to have an affair, Heather Strand. You're going to marry me. On my terms."

10

THE ROAD BACK to Tucson was virtually devoid of traffic. It stretched ahead of Heather and Jake, an endless strip of blacktop that was relatively unremarkable when one was in a car. On foot, it looked like the highway to eternity.

"It's really just a few miles," Heather pointed out bracingly. "And at least it's stopped raining. I'll try out my old hitchhiking skills on the first car that comes along."

"I'm sure you'll charm it to a stop, just like you charm everyone and everything else when you want to," Jake grumbled.

"Everyone except you, hmm?"

That brought a reluctant smile from him. "Oh, I'm as much under your spell as everyone else. I've told you that."

"Always nice to hear."

"The only difference with me is that I can handle you on the occasions when you decide not to be charming."

"I love it when you talk so masterfully. Listen! I hear something."

Jake swung around to glance back over his shoulder. "We're in luck. A truck. Now if we can just get him to stop."

"He'll stop," Heather promised, moving out into the road and waving her arms in a hopeful manner.

"Heather, cut that out. Let me handle this, will you?" Irritably, Jake yanked her back onto the shoulder of the road. "There's no need to flaunt yourself. After this kind of storm I'm sure the driver will realize we really do need a ride without you flinging yourself onto the hood of the truck."

"I just hope he hasn't already picked up a couple of other hitchhikers," Heather muttered meaningfully.

"Monroe and his pal? Not likely. If they made it through last night they'll probably be driving one of the jeeps out of the canyon. We've got to notify the cops as soon as possible. Chances are they're headed for the border."

There had been no sign of any life on the opposite side of the canyon that morning when Jake and Heather had hiked out. They were too far downstream to be able to tell if the jeeps were still parked near the Strands' cabin or even if the cabin itself had survived.

As Jake had predicted, the driver of the pickup stopped willingly enough, regaling them with stories of storm-caused damages he'd seen that morning. Heather climbed gratefully onto the worn seat and sat between the driver and Jake who gave a somewhat edited account of their own adventures.

"Not too smart to go up into these canyons when a thunderstorm's brewin'," the thin aging rancher advised with a sidelong glance at Jake.

"It wasn't my idea," Jake retorted dryly.

Heather endured the accusing glances of both men with equanimity. "Actually, I'm a runaway bride," she said chattily. "I left Jake standing at the altar the other day and he came after me."

The weatherbeaten rancher looked disconcerted and cast a questioning look at Jake.

"It's true," Jake sighed, sinking more deeply in the seat. "Unfortunately. I had visions of spending my honeymoon in Santa Fe, not that blasted canyon."

"It wasn't a honeymoon because we never did get married," Heather pointed out carefully. "We may never get married. Jake has decided he doesn't love me," she confided.

"Shut up, Heather."

"He's very bossy at times," Heather went on cheerfully.

"Heather...."

"You hear that warning tone in his voice? He sounds that way just before he lays down the law," she explained to the confused rancher.

"Heather, if you don't close your mouth I will do it for you."

Heather smiled devastatingly and said nothing for the remainder of the trip.

BY THE TIME the authorities had been notified of the activities of Monroe and his pal, Joe, it was midafternoon. A phone call earlier had assured Ruth and Paul Strand that everyone was safe, but Jake had made the call and Heather didn't actually have to face her parents or talk to them until late in the afternoon. As Jake parked the rental car in the private parking area of the hotel, much of her earlier breezy assurance faded.

"Oh, Jake. What am I going to say to them?" she groaned.

"Just tell them to reschedule the wedding for two weeks from today. The day before they leave on their cruise," Jake pointed out heartlessly as he opened the car door.

"I'm serious, Jake."

"So am I. That's what I'm going to tell them."

"To reschedule everything for two weeks from today? You'd better not unless you want to find yourself standing alone at the altar again!"

He turned to look at her as she remained sitting in the front seat of the car. The cool gray eyes were level and utterly unyielding. "You'll be there this time, Heather. Believe me." He straightened, slammed the door and came around to her side of the car. Without a word they walked toward her parents' home.

Ruth Strand appeared in the doorway, an anxious expression on her face as she watched Jake and Heather walking toward her. "Oh, Heather, darling. We were so worried. That storm was so violent and those canyons can be so treacherous!"

"I'm fine, Mom." Tears sprang into Heather's eyes as she ran toward her mother. "I'm fine. Oh, Mom, I'm so sorry for that awful scene the other day. It was stupid, childish and...and..." She hugged Ruth as she ran out of words.

"And you had every right to be absolutely furious," Ruth Strand said quiet firmly. "I was myself. Come on inside, you two. You need some hot coffee."

"Heather!" Paul Strand came hurrying in from the terrace. "Are you and Jake okay? I was really worried about the two of you up in that canyon last night." He glanced at Jake.

"The storm proved the least of our worries," Jake told the older man wryly. "Leave it to Heather to do everything with a bit of flair."

By the time he had told the Strands the whole story, Ruth and Paul had virtually forgotten the embarrassing event of the wedding. As she listened to his account of the tale, it occurred to Heather that Jake was going into the story in such detail precisely because he was trying to deflect the Strands' focus to it rather than to the wedding scene.

"I wouldn't have believed she had such stubborn strength in her," Jake said at one point, his gaze roving over Heather's figure as she sat sipping coffee at the kitchen table. "I told her to let go and, as usual, she just ignored instructions. There wasn't anything else I could do except climb out of that stream. It was obvious she wasn't going to give up."

"You should have seen Jake in the middle of a full-scale brawl," Heather put in quickly, uncomfortable under the cool admiration in his eyes. "Honestly, you would never have believed that in real life he's a mild-mannered hotel financier! I have a hunch they don't teach that sort of thing in accounting classes."

"Don't you believe it," Jake said calmly.

Ruth and Paul looked stunned by the whole tale. "Incredible. After all these years that punk Monroe showed up again," Paul murmured.

"I don't know for certain what he was using the cabin for but it sounded like it was a rendezvous point for his drug deals. Last night he kept saying he was going to be worth a fortune. We told the police everything we could and they're going to watch the border. Rick kept saying he was going to head for Mexico."

"And take you with him." Ruth shuddered in horror.

"Jake put a stop to that," Heather observed gently.

"And had to abandon your car in the process, Ruth." Jake sounded apologetic. "Tomorrow morning we'll drive back up that canyon and see what's left of the Mercedes and your sports car."

"Just as long as the two of you are okay, that's all that matters," Ruth assured him in heartfelt tones.

There was a moment of silence as everyone considered that. It was Paul who broke it with the one remaining unanswered question. Calmly he glanced from Jake's face to Heather's.

"Well? What are you two going to do now?"

"Go to work," Heather said with a calm that equaled her father's. "Jake and I are going to run the Hacienda, aren't we, Jake?"

"We work very well together," Jake agreed coolly. "We found that out for certain last night. So well, in fact, that we're going to go ahead and reschedule the wedding. I thought two weeks from today would do nicely." He watched Heather over the rim of his coffee cup, daring her to contradict him.

"Jake knows the conditions under which I'll marry him. If he's met those conditions by two weeks from today, we'll be married." She smiled blandly but her pulse was picking up uncomfortably. She had made herself into a challenge for him and intuition warned her that it was a foolish move on her part. Heather wasn't at all certain she could win in a deadly serious contest of wills with this man. Not when her own willpower was going to be undermined by the fact that she loved him with all her heart.

"Don't worry, Ruth," Jake said politely. "Heather will be at the wedding."

Paul and Ruth Strand looked from Heather to Jake and back again, silently weighing their knowledge of their daughter's stubborn pride against their knowledge of Jake's uncompromising determination.

Heather didn't care for the way either of her parents' mouths relaxed into a satisfied smile.

HEATHER HAD DINNER with Jake and her parents that night. She helped her mother prepare the tacos and enchiladas, working in a companionable manner that was very soothing to Heather's heightened state of tension. The readiness with which her parents seemed willing to forgive the scene with the motorcycle astonished her, but as Ruth kept saying, she fully sympathized with her daughter.

"Your note in the suitcase meant a lot, Mom. I felt so terrible about that scene once I'd had a chance to cool down and think it all over."

"I was astounded that those two would mislead you that way. I knew Paul intended to sell the Hacienda eventually but I thought he and Jake would strike a deal after the two of you were married." Ruth shook her head as she arranged the enchilada filling inside the tortillas. "Men. They always think they know what's best. Paul told me that he thought everything was all right because Jake had assured him he would be marrying you." She cast a sidelong glance at her daughter who was grating cheese. "Are you going to marry him in two weeks?"

"One way or another I'll be with Jake here on the Hacienda. He needs me."

"And you love him?"

"I love him. But I don't know if we'll be married in two weeks."

"Are you trying to punish him for what he did to you?" Ruth asked gently.

Heather firmly denied that with a shake of her head. "No. I'm trying to make him understand exactly how he feels about me. Jake doesn't know much about love. He doesn't trust it. He prefers to put his faith in other things like common interests and . . . and physical attraction."

"There is that last item between you two, isn't there?" Ruth chuckled. "You can tell a mile away. The two of you are so . . . so *aware* of each other. I know the feeling because your father and I have always had it."

Heather blinked, eyeing her mother in astonishment. "You don't seem particularly worried about the fact that that may be Jake's only interest in me."

"You're not eighteen anymore," Ruth replied shrugging. "I've seen my very successful, very intelligent daughter in action. She's an adult and she's learned to take care of herself. You and I have stepped out of the mother-daughter relationship. We're friends now, Heather. Good friends, I hope."

"The best," Heather agreed huskily, throwing her arms around her parent. "The best of friends."

The two women nugged each other in a silence that put the seal on the very special relationship that can only exist between mother and daughter.

After dinner Jake took Heather's arm in an almost painfully firm grasp as they started back through the hotel gardens.

"Well, you've certainly managed to earn everyone's forgiveness for standing me up at the wedding," he observed as he led her through the quiet grounds. "How do you do it, Heather? Magic?"

"Nope, not this time. You did it and you know it. You had everyone so grateful that I was alive that they forgot to be angry at me for having caused that scene. I owe you one, Jake."

He smiled. "Good. Maybe if I get you deep enough in debt you won't cause me any trouble in a couple of weeks when it's time to drag you to the altar."

Heather paused, obliging him to stop beside her. Her mouth curved upward as she lifted her face in the moonlight. The desert skies were clear again and the sparkling night was warm and inviting.

"I love you, Jake."

He groaned and pulled her close, crushing her mouth hungrily beneath his own. "Then don't fight me," he urged against her lips. "Don't fight me."

"I won't fight you tonight. Shall I come back to your cottage with you?" She traced a pattern against the nape of his neck, her fingers moving tantalizingly there. Her body arched closer to his, full of invitation and responsive desire.

Jake lifted his head, eyes shadowed and gleaming in the night. "A week ago I'd have stumbled over my own feet accepting the offer."

"Tired of me already?"

"You know very well that's not the case. The way I feel I could put you down right here on the grass and take you," he grated.

She could feel the physical tension in his body and knew he was telling the truth. "I'm not fighting you, Jake. You're fighting me."

"Do you think that if you seduce me often enough I'll give you what you want?" he asked bitterly. "It won't work, Heather. Stop playing your dramatic little games and act like the woman I know you are."

Heather tried to hide the hurt she knew must be reflected in her eyes. She pulled her arms free from around his neck. "Good night, Jake. I'll see you in the morning."

Jake set his teeth angrily as she disappeared through the dimly lit garden. Then he grimly followed, watching from a discreet distance as she let herself safely into her cottage. He'd hurt her with that last crack about playing games, he realized. It was odd to have the power to hurt someone. He didn't think he'd ever possessed that kind of power before and it made him uncomfortable.

He was made considerably more uncomfortable by the stark loneliness of his bed. Two nights of having Heather in his arms had apparently spoiled him completely.

"Cavender," he muttered savagely to himself as he lay staring at the ceiling, "you're an idiot." The situation was ridiculous. They both wanted each other; they both intended to stay together. What the hell was he doing letting her play games with him like this? The fastest way out of the impasse would be to push her into realizing that she had no real choice in the matter. She'd never had any choice. Not since the first time he'd met her. She had been visiting her parents over the Christmas holidays and he'd looked at her and known he would have her and the Hacienda. Everything would be perfect. He'd have a complete home with a wife who understood him and wanted the same things out of life that he did.

A home. That thought lingered in his head for a tantalizing moment.

Everything had gone so well until that scene at the chapel. Even after that he thought he'd gotten matters back under control. She wanted him and she wanted the Hacienda. What could be simpler than marrying him?

Perhaps it was all his own fault for having freed the passionate side of her nature. He hadn't intended to do that until after the wedding, but he'd pushed her too far when he'd hidden the full truth about ownership of the Hacienda from her. Discovering the way she had been deliberately misled had burst the bonds holding her basic nature in check. Making love to her afterward had only served to heighten the effect. Her surrender had been as deeply passionate as her anger. A formidable combination.

Jake had never felt so utterly determined in his life as he did in that moment. He would put a halt to Heather's dramatic little fantasy of love and force her to accept the situation between them for what it was. After all, there was still that practical businesslike side of her nature to tap. He'd use it to resolve the conflict between them.

The decision made, Jake climbed out of bed, stepped into a pair of jeans and padded barefoot to his desk. Sitting down, he switched on the lamp and opened the drawer. He pulled out a copy of the prenuptial agreement he'd signed and began to study it in detail. Then he reached for another sheet of paper and a pen.

By the time he was finished with her, Heather was going to acknowledge that their relationship wasn't a romantic fantasy built on froth and pink air. It was a solid unbreakable association based on sturdy unwavering grounds.

Heather could save the dramatic passionate side of her nature for the bedroom. Other than there, it had no place in the business of their marriage.

An hour later when he'd finished his task he was far too alert and restless to sleep. Jake put on some canvas shoes and slipped out into the silent gardens to have a late-night chat with security.

HEATHER FELT unaccountably suspicious of the dinner invitation from the moment she accepted it the following afternoon. But she dressed for the occasion that evening with panache. The dress she chose was one she had brought with her from San Francisco. It was a close-fitting white sheath, ornamented with dazzling sequined roses on the squared shoulders. With any luck, she told herself, the draped vee neckline was cut low enough to intrigue Jake's attention but not so low as to earn her a lecture. Heather sighed inwardly as she turned away from the mirror. She certainly walked a fine line these days.

She knew a strange kind of tension lately, as if she was on a ragged edge between surrender and resistance. Logically she believed she was following the right course of action. Her whole future with Jake depended on maintaining it. But there was a deep need inside her to cease the struggle and simply throw herself into

Jake's arms. She loved him. She didn't want to do battle with him.

How long could this nerve-racking situation go on, she wondered bleakly. It was one thing to manage a male employee. Quite another to manage the man who held your heart in the palm of his hand.

So much depended on the groundwork she was trying to lay, she told herself again and again. She must be strong.

Jake was at her door promptly at six-thirty looking a little on the sober, restrained side. The dark aloofness in him ought to have been offset by the cream-colored sport coat he wore with the open-necked coffee-colored shirt and slacks. But as usual, his clothing didn't affect the overall impression of self-imposed distance. Heather couldn't stand it. She knew him too intimately to be put off by the impression.

The moment she opened the door she stepped forward, rose on tiptoe and brushed her mouth across his with sweet warmth. "I hear we'll be able to go in the Mercedes tonight," she said lightly, stepping away before Jake could respond. "Dad says you and he and someone from the grounds-keeping staff drove up into the canyon to rescue the cars."

"They were both covered with mud but otherwise okay." Jake's eyes lingered for a moment on the vee of the white sheath. "That dress is cut a bit low, isn't it?"

"No." Heather smiled brightly and closed the front door behind her. "Any sign of the jeeps Rick and his friend drove?"

"None," he answered as they walked toward the parking lot. "It looks as though they made it out of the canyon. With any luck the authorities will nab them at the border."

"I hope so," Heather agreed fervently. "Where are we going tonight?"

"Someplace we can talk."

"Well, that's encouraging. Talk about us, you mean?" she tried for a cheerful note, anxious not to let any of her trepidation show.

"About us," he confirmed.

He drove to an elegant restaurant in the hills overlooking the city, saying little en route. Heather sensed that he was involved with his own musings and she longed to be able to read his mind. Had he thought about their untenable situation? she wondered nervously. Perhaps he had reached the decision she wanted him to reach. Perhaps he had accepted the fact that he was in love with her. The jumbled hopes and fears in her own head kept her unusually silent on the drive. It was after Jake had parked the Mercedes in the lot of the restaurant and guided her firmly indoors into the elegant Spanish-colonial decor that she realized matters were not going to end rosily that evening.

"Let's have a drink first," he ordered, taking her into the darkened, quiet lounge and leading her to a small table for two. "A glass of burgundy?"

"You know me so well," she murmured, trying for a small joke."

"Better than you know yourself," he agreed far too seriously. He ordered a Scotch for himself and watched her in silence as the drinks were delivered.

Heather moved uneasily under the intent regard and then forced herself to sit coolly still. When the wine arrived she was grateful, however, to have something to do with her restless hands. Jake was in a dangerous mood tonight and she knew it. There was a hard relentless determination in the depths of those gray eyes that disturbed her. In this mood he was virtually unmanageable.

"Now, then," he began after letting the silence between them grow to huge dimensions, "I think it's time we got down to business."

"Business?" She heard the wariness in her own voice and knew he must have heard it too.

"Business. You don't want to be my wife—"

"I never said that," she protested urgently.

"Let me rephrase that. You insist that any marriage between us be on your terms. Terms I find unacceptable."

Heather's mouth went dry.

"Since marriage is therefore out of the question, we are left with another sort of situation entirely. You are willing to work for the Hacienda and perform the function of being my mistress. I never have anyone working for me who doesn't have a clear concept of his or her responsibilities. I find it saves a lot of trouble if the position is clearly understood right from the beginning. I have therefore drawn up a contract that covers your chosen job duties."

Heather's fingers closed too tightly around the stem of her wineglass. Without a word she took a deep swallow of burgundy and watched in morbid fascination as Jake withdrew a folded document from inside his cream-colored jacket. When he handed it to her she was forced to lower the wineglass and accept it.

A horrible sense of déjà vu struck her as her hand closed over the document. Memories of the prenuptial agreement she had insisted Jake sign were burning in her head, and she knew her eyes probably gave away her thoughts. Quickly she lowered her lashes to hide the humiliation and chagrin.

"You've been busy," she tried to say offhandedly, staring unseeingly at the neatly typed clauses on the two-page document in front of her. At that moment she couldn't read a word.

"I drafted it last night and typed it myself this morning. I'll want your signature on it by the first of next week, Heather."

"I see." Unsteadily she refolded the contract and shoved it into her sequined purse. *My God,* she thought dazedly, *he's going to pin me to the wall like a butterfly.*

"Aren't you going to read it?" Jake prodded blandly.

"Later. I'll want to study it in some detail, I'm sure." She tried another sip of burgundy in an effort to bring her fragmented pulse under control.

"I'll be glad to outline the main points."

No, she wanted to scream, *don't outline a damn thing. I don't want to hear it. I don't want to hear you outline a contract for my love.* "Feel free," she heard herself invite calmly.

He leaned forward, holding the glass of Scotch in one tanned hand. The candlelight flickered on the liquor in his glass, making the stuff look like molten gold. Heather focused on it.

"Basically what that contract says is that you're my employee. You'll work for me and you'll answer only to me. You will follow orders in the same professional manner as any good employee, keeping in mind that what I want for the Hacienda Strand is what you want."

"The perfect yes-woman?"

"Not exactly. You will be assuming the role of my personal assistant and as such, I don't object to hearing your opinion on matters. But an occasional opinion or suggestion is all I want from you. No arguments, undisciplined battles or emotional protests. You are not sharing ownership of the Hacienda with me as you would if you were my wife. You are merely an employee of the corporation."

Heather closed her eyes in brief pain but forced herself to open them almost immediately.

"I have stipulated what I think is a reasonable salary and you will continue to receive the use of your cottage as part of your compensation."

"The Hacienda has always been my home," she said quietly. "It will be difficult to think in terms of renting my cottage." The truth was, it would be almost impossible and she suspected Jake knew it.

"The Hacienda is no more your home than it is that of any of the employees," Jake said evenly.

"Will you be charging my parents rent, too?"

"Your parents and I have an entirely unrelated understanding. My agreement with them has nothing to do with the one I'm establishing with you."

"Oh."

"Where was I?" Jake continued relentlessly, his voice ow and hard. "Yes. I remember. In addition to functioning as my personal assistant you will also perform the duties of hostess for the Hacienda. It's obviously something you're good at and I need those skills. Above all you will keep in mind that your only goal is to carry out my wishes."

"Will you be standing over me with whips and chains?" she challenged tightly.

"I don't think there will be any need for that. You've proven over the past few years that you are more than capable of a high level of professional behavior. I'm asking only for that same professionalism now. So much for the first half of the contract."

"I can't wait to hear the second half." Heather gulped more wine, her eyes burning.

"The second half relates to your duties as my mistress."

"Your lover," she corrected distantly.

"For purposes of the contract, the word is *mistress*. As I've told you before, it would be extremely awkward for me to have you living with me. As owner of the Hacienda I feel obliged to maintain a certain image."

"You mean you think it might be a bit tacky to be sleeping openly with the daughter of the former owner?" Heather asked bitterly.

"Very tacky. There will, however, be occasions for business trips, vacations, weekends away, that sort of thing. I will expect you to travel with me at those times."

"That's not tacky?"

"At the moment you're functioning as my employee. Save the flippancy for some other occasion."

"I thought I was out on a date with you," she remarked wistfully.

"This is business. And because being my mistress is just another job, I am willing to pay a separate salary."

Heather went white. With extreme care she set down her glass of wine, not trusting herself to be able to hold it any longer.

Watching her from across the table Jake faltered. He was crucifying her and he knew it. But in the end it would be less painful to push her like this than to allow her to manipulate both of them with her unrealistic, passionately romantic, highly emotional approach.

"It doesn't have to be like this, Heather," he growled gently, stretching out a hand to capture her too-still fingers.

"Doesn't it?" She stared at him, her wounded stricken face drawn in the candlelight.

"You know it doesn't. Stop playing games and marry me. It's as simple as that. You'll share ownership of the Hacienda with me and you'll share my life. It's what both of us want."

"It's not enough," she told him evenly. "Not nearly enough. I won't tie myself to a man who doesn't know how to love."

Jake's face tightened. "Damn it, Heather, you're tied to me one way or another, can't you see that? Why do it the hard way?"

"Asking you to love me as much as I love you is the hard way?"

"Heather, I know you want—" Jake broke off abruptly, his eyes lifting to a point just above her left shoulder. "Oh, hell."

"What is it?"

"Cecil and Connie Winthrop."

"How lovely. You can make a full business meeting out of our date, can't you?" Heather breathed bitterly.

"Invite them over and you can make another pitch to buy their land for your precious golf-course project."

Jake's gaze flicked back to her tense face. "Why not? And since it's going to be one of your assignments to get me that land, I'll let you handle the whole thing." He rose to his feet.

"Jake, wait...."

He ignored the pleading in her eyes as he signaled to the Winthrops. "Just remember that I want that land, Heather."

"But we haven't really discussed the golf course."

"I'm not obliged to discuss anything with my personal assistant unless I so choose. Get me that land, Heather."

Before she could protest further, the Winthrops were upon them, beaming down at Heather with avid curiosity and a hint of amusement in their eyes. Heather tried an uneasy smile, aware of the fact that the Winthrops had undoubtedly been among the two hundred or so guests present at the chapel a few mornings earlier.

"Heather, darling, we heard you and Jake had a fascinating little adventure up in one of the canyons. You were so very lucky, you know," Connie Winthrop gushed cheerfully. "Those canyon streams and rivers can be so tricky during our stormy season. But your mother said Jake was with you? . . ." She turned her inquiring gaze on the abandoned groom, clearly alive with curiosity.

Jake gave the graying, middle-aged woman his familiar half smile and assisted her into a chair. "I could hardly allow Heather to go haring off alone into those mountains. How are you, Cecil?" He extended his hand politely to Cecil Winthrop who shook it readily.

"Fine, just fine. I might ask the same question of you, young man. It sounds to me as if our Heather has been giving you a hard time lately."

"Cecil!" his wife admonished hurriedly.

"I think I'll survive," Jake murmured, his gaze on Heather's face. "Things have been a little rocky lately, but basically Heather and I understand each other. We're getting it all ironed out, aren't we, honey?"

"Matters between us are being steamrollered, not neatly ironed out," Heather responded with a shred of her natural spirit. She turned to Connie Winthrop with her most brilliant smile. Jake said he wanted that land. Very well, she would get it for him.

11

FRIDAY MORNING, three days later, Jake stood in the doorway of the office Heather had taken over and watched as she pored over a new menu Julian Richards was seeking permission to implement. Heather's whole attention was on the list of ingredients the Hacienda would have to inventory in order to present the menu day in and day out. The logistics of running a hotel restaurant were enormous and the cost of maintaining fresh foods was high. She was so wrapped up in the project that she hadn't even noticed him lounging in the doorway.

Ever since the night he had taken her out to dinner she had been like this, Jake reflected. Totally involving herself in work, she was spending up to sixteen hours a day in the office. It was unnerving to see the kind of energy she could funnel into work.

Warily he had tried a few business conversations with her but Heather had merely listened politely, nodding agreement to everything he said. She had volunteered no input whatsoever. He could see the tension under which she was living and the knowledge that he was the cause of it was eating at him night and day. How much longer before she broke?

No, Jake told himself savagely, he didn't want to break her, only make her bend for both their sakes. But at the rate matters were progressing it was possible he would collapse first. That thought brought a wry grimace to his mouth just as Heather became aware of his presence.

"Good morning, Jake. I didn't hear you."

"Obviously." He tried a smile and wasn't certain how well it came out. "Does the menu look at all feasible?"

"I think we can handle it with a few small changes. Julian has his heart set on upgrading the wine cellar, too. It's going to cost us . . . you, a fortune."

He heard the way she tripped over the word *us* and swore inwardly. "I just had a call from Cecil Winthrop."

"Did you?"

"He's going to accept our . . . my offer on that land."

Heather nodded, saying nothing. She turned back to the menu.

"You're the reason he and Connie finally agreed to sell," Jake went on doggedly.

"You can show your appreciation by throwing in a Christmas bonus."

"Heather!"

That brought her head up, her hazel eyes flashing with a familiar vividness, which she managed to subdue almost instantly. "I'm sorry, Jake. I forgot myself. I'm a little tired this morning."

He surveyed the coffee cup beside her desk and noted that the office pot was already half-empty. "You're drinking too much coffee lately."

Heather glared at him, about to make a crack about paying for the coffee herself if he was so concerned about expenses, but something stopped her. His tone had been gruff but not genuinely annoyed. Surely he wasn't actually worried about her physical well-being, she scoffed silently. And then, quite suddenly, she knew he was. Their glances clashed across the width of the room.

"I'll switch to tea," she heard herself offer.

"Try milk."

"Impossible. I detest milk." Heather smiled wryly. "Not even for you will I switch to milk."

"There are a lot of things you aren't willing to do for me."

"Only one or two," she corrected with a totally false cheeriness. *Like marry you or switch to milk. Just a couple of things.* Heather wondered gloomily how long she would be able to continue this silent war of wills.

Jake straightened and moved toward her desk purposefully. He settled himself casually on the edge, one leg bracing his weight against the floor. "How much longer, Heather?" he asked softly.

"Until I sign the contract? You gave me until Monday, remember?"

"You know it's not what you want."

"I know." Her smile was sad and a little whimsical. "Excuse me, Jake. I've got to get back to work. Julian needs an answer on these menus so he can contact suppliers."

Jake's mouth firmed into a grin. Heather knew he wanted to say something else but he changed his mind at the last minute. Without a word he removed himself from her desk and her office.

As soon as she heard the door close behind him Heather's body went limp as if from complete exhaustion. She dropped her head into her hands and closed her eyes against the incipient tears. How much longer? They were tearing each other apart.

It was becoming increasingly clear to her that she wasn't the only one suffering. Jake hid his tension and frustrated anger behind a facade of remote, cool detachment, but she knew the remorseless situation was affecting him.

Slowly Heather raised her head and reached into the middle drawer of her desk for the contract. It seemed to burn her fingers as she pulled it out and stared down at the savage clauses for the hundredth time.

If she signed it she would be committing both herself and Jake to an endless siege. Neither of them wanted the kind of situation outlined in that document.

If she gave in and tore it up, agreed to marry Jake, she would be abandoning the fight and the goal she had set. She would be agreeing to tie herself to a man who might never learn to give himself completely; never learn to love.

It had all been so simple when she had thought it was just the Hacienda that was truly important. But the Hacienda Strand had become insignificant the moment she had acknowledged her love for Jake. As for Jake, he was still trying to have it all and on his own terms.

His own terms. Heather ached when she thought of the words. Wasn't that what she was trying to do? Have it all on her own terms. Except for her the only thing she really wanted was Jake's love and total commitment.

Simple. And devastating.

"Heather?"

She turned awkwardly at the sound of Paul Strand's voice. "Oh, hi Dad. On your way to a golf game?"

"Where else?" He sauntered into the office wearing lime-green slacks and a watermelon-colored knit shirt.

"Your mother found this for me the other day. I'm going to take it with me on the cruise. What do you think?"

"That you'll be stoned in Scotland. I thought mother had better taste than that."

Paul grimaced. "So did I. She claims we have to spruce up our wardrobes for the cruising life-style."

"Well, she's often been right in the past. Maybe you should go ahead and trust her judgment."

Paul gave her a searching glance. "I used to think I could trust my own, too. But lately I've had some serious doubts. I just passed Jake in the lobby."

"Did you?" Heather started to shuffle some papers on her desk.

"He looks the way he used to look when he first came here, Heather. Ever since he decided to buy the place and marry you he's been changing. During the past month he was almost out of his shell. Now he looks as though he was engaged in a war."

"I'm beginning to think that's the way he views our current situation," Heather remarked dryly.

"What the hell are you doing to him, honey?" Paul's voice dropped to the roughly affectionate note he used around her when they weren't at odds.

"I wish I knew. I thought I was trying to force him into realizing certain truths about us. But his instincts are to fight back when he's challenged. He's going to beat me to a pulp, Dad," she concluded in humorless amusement.

Her father frowned. "He knows damn well that if he ever laid a hand on you, I'd kill him."

Some of Heather's amusement became briefly real. "Would you? That man's almost become a son to you."

"A father respects his son but he looks after his daughter. At least until the right man comes along to take care of her. Jake's the right man, Heather. I've known that for the past year and a half. I know I was wrong to agree to keep the sale of the Hacienda quiet until after the wedding. But I knew Jake was afraid you'd run out on him if you thought you weren't going to gain control of the hotel. He insisted the Hacienda had to be bait. Frankly, I was inclined to agree with him. I didn't think you'd ever come home unless you had the lure of inheriting this place. He was right on that score, wasn't he? You did run when you found out you weren't going to assume the presidency of the corporation."

"I ran because I felt like a fool. I felt betrayed."

"Heather, honey, I never meant—"

She waved off his earnest apology and explanation. "It doesn't matter, Dad. I'm over that. I started getting over it when it was forcibly pointed out to me that I'd really been very arrogant and rather unintelligent about the whole thing."

"Jake said that?"

"Umm. That was after the wedding. He was a trifle upset after having been stood up at the altar, I gather," Heather confessed wryly.

Her father nodded. "We all were. Your mother read both Jake and I the riot act. The next morning—" Paul continued hesitantly "—the next morning when he returned on that motorcycle he said he was going to give you a little time. I watched him pace the office for over two hours before he finally decided he wasn't going to give you any time. By then the storm clouds were moving in and when I found out you were taking your breather up at the old cabin I mentioned that might not be the wisest place in which to be during a summer storm. He asked to borrow Ruth's car and the next thing I knew I was drawing him a map. He was gone within fifteen minutes."

"And arrived in time to rescue me," Heather finished for him. "Don't look at me like that, Dad. I love him."

Her father eyed her uncertainly. "Then what in heaven's name is all this warfare about?"

Heather stared at her father and knew she could never explain that the man he had chosen and groomed for her didn't love her. "We're, uh, having to work a few things out before we tie any knots."

Paul looked at her with gentle sympathy and a trace of pity. "You mean you're at war with him. Heather, I know better than anyone else on the face of this earth just how stubborn and strong you are. Do you think I haven't been incredibly proud of what you accomplished in California? Do you think I don't realize what it cost you to make it the hard way out there? But I've also learned a lot about Jake Cavender during the past couple of years. And believe me, if one of you doesn't give you're going to draw a lot of blood. In the end, you'll be the one who will be in shreds."

"Because he's stronger than I am?" Heather asked softly.

Paul shook his head. "Because he simply won't ever give in. You were right. His instincts are to fight when he's challenged and his instincts were tempered in a much hotter furnace than yours were, honey. You can fight like a wildcat, but there's a softness in you."

"Because I grew up with love."

"It makes you able to bend when necessary. Jake can't give like that."

"I'm beginning to understand that," Heather admitted simply, knowing the truth of her father's words had been creeping up on her for the past four days.

"If you didn't love him you might have a chance of winning a pitched battle. But loving him...." Paul shrugged unhappily. "I just wish to God I had realized what I was starting two years ago when I hired the man."

Heather shook her head, her eyes softening. "Even if you knew, you'd have gone ahead and hired him. You always were a good judge of character. Do you think I haven't come to realize that?"

"I love you, Heather."

"And I love you, Dad."

"We've always had that bond, haven't we?" Paul asked gently.

Heather smiled, dashing the back of her hand across her eyes. "Always. Jake's never had that kind of attachment to any living human being, as far as I can tell."

"Perhaps not. On the other hand—" Paul announced, as he kissed his daughter on the cheek and headed for the door "—the guy's not exactly stupid. See you later, Heather."

Not exactly stupid. Heather repeated the words to herself and shook her head once again. It was true Jake wasn't an idiot, but she wasn't so sure about herself. Refolding the contract, Heather went back to work on the menus.

ON SATURDAY Heather politely declined an invitation from her mother to join her parents and Jake for dinner. Ruth Strand didn't press the issue. She knew a woman under pressure when she saw one.

Heather spent the evening alone, fixing herself a salad and a glass of wine. Then she put her jeaned legs beneath her on the sofa and carefully unfolded the contract Jake had dared her to sign. Her father was right. Ultimately, she had the capacity to bend. Jake didn't. If she signed this contract Jake would be denied everything he wanted including the feeling of having a real home with a real wife. The relationship with Paul and Ruth that he valued so highly would never again be as warm and comfortable as it was now. He had ownership of the Hacienda but he wouldn't have achieved the feeling of really belonging to it. And Jake didn't want a mistress. He wanted a wife.

All the trappings of a family together with a feeling of a home.

Heather had told herself that was precisely what she wanted. She had been able to tell herself that until the morning she had realized she was in love with Jake. After that the only thing that had mattered was obtaining his love in return

Jake wanted a partner; she wanted a passionate life-long love affair. Jake could go on playing manipulative games indefinitely. She loved him and knew that for her the attempts to manipulate Jake couldn't go on much longer. She was hurting both of them too badly in the process and in the end, as her father had said, she would be the one in shreds. Love left you vulnerable.

It was nearly ten o'clock. Heather made her decision and got to her feet. Outside thunder rolled overhead. Another late-night storm. The sound of its approach reminded her of the canyon and the night she had spent with Jake. She could not go on battling the man she loved.

Slipping her bare feet into a pair of sandals, Heather opened the door. It hadn't yet started raining. No need to throw a waterproof jacket on over the wide-sleeved, narrow-cuffed artist's shirt she wore. Hurrying, Heather went down the steps to her porch and headed for the garden path that led to Jake's cottage. With any luck he would be home from her parents' house by now.

There was a golden glow behind the curtains as Heather raised her hand to knock firmly on the door. It was only after she had committed herself by knocking that Heather experienced a rush of uncertainty.

That uncertainty vanished a moment later as Jake opened the door and stood staring down at her.

"Heather?" The gray eyes narrowed and he seemed to tense as if for battle. "What are you doing here?"

"I thought we should discuss this contract." She held up the folded document, trying desperately to stem the conflicting emotions flooding her bloodstream.

Jake's gaze went to the contract and back to her face and never in the entire time she had known him had he seemed more remote or, in some indefinable way, more dangerous. "I see. Come in."

She stepped through the door just as the rain started to come down in torrents. He closed the door and stood with his back to it, watching her with an intensity that shook her to the core. She turned to face him, holding the contract in both hands.

"What exactly did you want to discuss? Have you signed it?"

"No, I haven't signed it."

The relief that flashed into his eyes disappeared almost immediately but Heather had seen it and her love for him washed through her, destroying any lingering doubts.

Very deliberately she smiled and tore the contract in half. He watched, utterly fascinated, as she turned it sideways and ripped it into quarters. Then she stepped toward him and dropped the bits of the document onto the floor at his feet.

"I love you, Jake. I couldn't possibly sign that silly contract." Her arms went around his neck and she pulled his head down toward hers.

"Heather!"

Her name was a rasping cry against her mouth. She heard untrammeled relief, gratitude and some exultation, but she didn't think she heard the resounding note of victory. In any event Heather wasn't paying much attention.

Jake pulled her into the strength of his body, his broad hands flattened along the length of her back and down to her hips as he sought to force every inch of her against him.

His tongue forged hungrily into her mouth, seeking the taste and warmth of her. Heather felt the force of the leaping desire in him and gave herself up to it with a willingness that stoked Jake's need to an even higher level.

"Heather, Heather! You'll marry me?"

"Yes."

He buried his lips in her hair, inhaling the scent of it. "I was so afraid you'd fight me until there was nothing left. That's why I pushed so hard, honey. Please try to understand. I had to force you to the wall. I never wanted to hurt you."

"I know, Jake," she soothed, translating the gentling tone of her voice to the tips of her fingers as she massaged the hard curve of his shoulders. "I know, darling. It's all right now. Everything is all right."

"Heather...."

"Shh. Don't say anything else. Not just now. Let me make love to you, Jake. Just let me make love to you."

"My God. Do you think I'd try to stop you? But you'll have to wait your turn. I've been aching for you these past few days. Aching so much I thought I'd go out of my mind."

"I wanted to feel your touch, my love. At night as I lay in bed alone I wondered if you would ever touch me like this again," she confessed softly.

"I'll be holding you like this for the rest of my life," he vowed fervently. With a husky groan he scooped her up and settled her onto the love seat. "Tonight I need you so badly I can't even take the time to carry you into the bedroom."

The feverish desire flared between them, cutting off any further conversation except for the urgent passionate murmurs that are a form of communication between lovers. Jake touched the fastenings of Heather's clothes with hands of magic. Her garments seemed to melt away from her body and she heard his husky ntake of breatn as nis paim cupped her oreast in gentle possession.

"Ah, Heather. My sweet Heather...."

His own clothes were removed with masculine impatience a moment later and then he came back down on top of her, covering her body with his own as he slid forcefully between her thighs.

Heather felt the heavy heat of him waiting to engulf her, and trembled. Jake lowered his head, taking her mouth in an all-consuming kiss. His hands moved down to her hips, squeezing the soft resilient curves of her body. She shivered again, lifting herself with silent invitation as he trailed his fingers through the fine hair of the dark triangle.

"Please, Jake. Oh, my darling love. . . ."

He nipped hungrily at the budding peak of her breast. "You're so incredibly responsive," he breathed, obviously luxuriating in the hot warmth of her.

"I never knew I could be like this," she said simply as her fingers urged him closer.

"Heather!" With a thick groan of desire, Jake thrust deeply into her soft feminine channel, uniting them in the act of love.

Heather shimmered under the overwhelming assault of Jake's body, giving herself to him with all the love and passion that had been set free during the trauma of their courtship.

When the white-hot intensity of their shared need consumed them both, Heather no longer cared whether Jake viewed her love in terms of surrender. She gave herself completely and in the process of giving received everything she could ever need or want.

Jake sealed the pact between them with the elemental fire of possession, and when Heather's body tightened beneath his, he joined her in the tumultuous completion, calling her name hoarsely as he sank deeply into her softness.

IT WAS A LONG TIME before Jake stirred lazily against the sweetly limp form entwined with his. Heather moved protestingly but didn't open her eyes. She nestled her tousled head into his shoulder and invited the smoothing movement of his hand with her tantalizingly curved hip.

"Cold?" he asked huskily.

"Umm."

"Does that mean yes or no?"

"Umm."

He smiled to himself and waited another few minutes, enjoying the feel of her leg as it lay trapped between his muscular thighs. She was so soft and capable of such passion. What had he ever done to deserve his present contentment?

The answer to that question slammed into his head with uncomfortable certainty. He'd fought for it. Harder than he'd fought for anything in his life. And he'd confronted a worthy opponent. If Heather hadn't surrendered tonight there was no telling where the fighting would have stopped.

A wave of irritation made him move, forcing him up to a sitting position. Heather murmured a catlike protest, this time opening her eyes.

"Getting ready to kick me out so soon, Jake?"

He scowled. "I'm not going to kick you out."

"Of course you are. You have your reputation to consider, remember?" She teased him with her eyes as she patted a small yawn. "Don't worry, I understand completely. Can't have the entire staff gossiping about us, can we?"

"I don't want them gossiping about you, honey."

She grinned. "Jake, the staff has always gossiped about me. I've been giving them stuff to talk about since the day I was born!"

"Well, not anymore," he declared roughly.

"Then you are going to kick me out?" She traced the line of his mouth with a copper-tipped finger.

"I'm going to walk you home before anyone realizes you've stayed too long."

Her eyes lit up with love and humor. "Are you going to be a tyrannical sort of husband, Jake?"

The word *husband* paused for a moment in his head and Jake examined it closely. Very seriously he looked down at Heather. "I'll try to be the best possible husband, honey. I'll take care of you, look after you."

"In other words, you'll be a tyrant." She rolled over so that her nude body flowed along the top of his.

"We're going to be partners, Heather," he corrected carefully, not sure what to make of her teasing.

"With you being the senior partner?"

"I want us to work together. You know that."

"And you also want a home."

His hands tightened around her bare waist and the gray depths of his eyes reflected the extent of his yearning. "I want a home with *you*, Heather."

"Your wish is my command," she murmured softly, dipping her head to kiss him lightly.

"Heather, what made you come here tonight?"

"You know the answer to that. I love you. And I want a home with you. I'd marry you regardless of whether or not the Hacienda came with the package."

"I know that," he whispered thickly, realizing he'd known that since the first time he'd made love to her. He tried to find the words to communicate the unsettled driving message in his mind, knowing that he had to get it across but not at all certain how to do it. "Honey, I've got to talk to you."

"So talk." She dropped another delicate kiss on his cheek.

"I should be taking you home." He didn't know how to tell her what he was feeling but he sensed it might take some time. They really didn't have time tonight. Nor did he have any champagne or roses or a romantic setting. He wanted to tell her in the right way. He wanted it to be perfect.

"If you're determined to take me back to the cottage, I suppose I'd better put some clothes on. If one of the security people saw me dashing naked through the rain there's no telling what sort of talk would be going down tomorrow. Your reputation would be in tatters!"

He sensed the reluctance in her as she pulled away from him and began scrabbling around on the floor for her clothing. Wonderingly he put out a hand and threaded his fingers through her sensually tossed hair as she bent over to pick up a shirt. When she swung a quick amused glance at him he caught his breath at the love shining out of her hazel eyes.

"Heather," he started in desperation, "I didn't want it to be like this. I didn't want surrender. . . ."

"I know," she responded simply. Then, before he could find the rest of the words, she was on her feet, tugging on her silky panties and the narrow-legged jeans.

Slowly he sat up, dazed by the emotional turmoil seething inside him. Never had he felt such conflicting frantic sensations. "I wanted . . . I didn't want a victory." Painfully he searched for the words.

Her eyes softened. "Better get dressed, darling, unless you want to be the one who walks naked back through the gardens."

He obeyed slowly, aware of the new tension in himself as he tried to sort it all out. He had to get this right.

"Heather, you won't regret this marriage. I swear it."

She was already at the door. "I know I won't regret it. How could I?"

"Honey, I'm trying to explain—"

"Oh, look, it's stopped raining. We won't get soaked preserving your image." She had the door opened and was peering out into the darkness.

Jake paused by the desk, opening a drawer and automatically removing the object inside. He caught up with Heather just as she stepped out into the night. Urgently he grasped her arm, aware that he had to say the rest of the words now, tonight. He had realized he didn't want victory the moment he'd seen her standing at his door this evening. He only wanted her. He just hadn't known how else to go about the task of ensuring her surrender.

No, damn it, he hadn't wanted her surrender. *What a lie, Cavender.* There was nothing else it could be called. Well, he'd had no choice, had he? He'd wanted an honest relationship, based on honest bonds. He'd longed for something real and solid between them, not ephemeral fantasies. His approach had all been for the best.

She'd surrendered so sweetly, he thought in shock as they walked silently back through the grounds. And he'd taken everything she had to give. He'd never had a woman who gave as completely of herself as Heather did. And she didn't seem to be bitter or resentful about the way he had pushed her until she'd given in.

A woman as passionate and headstrong as Heather should be railing at him, screaming her anger and frustration, trying to punish him for lacerating her pride. If the situation had been reversed he'd have....

No, there was no way the situation could have been reversed. He would never have been able to find the courage to surrender.

Surrender. The word was going to haunt him. He didn't like the taste of victory, Jake discovered. He wanted to give as much to Heather as she had given to him. Only that kind of mutual surrender could satisfy him.

"Heather, listen to me, I want to explain something. Something very important...."

The quickly moving storm clouds fled through the night sky, slipping past the moon. The pale light caught the length of the gun barrel just as the man crouched in the shadows beside Heather's front door raised the weapon and fired.

12

HEATHER NEVER SAW the man or the gun. One moment she was walking beside Jake, pleasantly aware of the feel of his hand on her arm, and the next she was plunging headfirst into the carefully tended shrubbery on her left. The propulsion power came from the hand with which Jake had been guiding her and it was followed by the full force of his body.

The unmistakable crack of a gunshot exploded in the darkness just as Jake shoved her forward. Heather felt the impact of something slamming into Jake even as he slammed into her, covering her body with his own.

"Jake!"

"Shut up," he hissed, his hand clamping over her mouth. She nodded quickly to show she understood and then he released her, rolling free of her body and realigning himself in the muddy shrub bed. She saw him digging into his belt and an instant later a small hand-gun appeared in his fist.

There was deadly silence from the shadows near Heather's porch. Jake scanned the bushes, telling himself to ignore the total lack of feeling in his right arm. Somewhere he'd read that it took a while for the pain of a bullet to make itself known. The body responded first with shocked numbness.

He was aware of Heather lying still beside him in the mud but he didn't turn to glance in her direction. From the direction of the main lodge he thought he heard a shout. That would be security.

A flash of light shot through the shadows followed instantly by another crack of sound. The bullet went wild. Willing himself to concentrate completely on the least trace of movement, Jake waited.

Rick Monroe broke cover a split second later. He must have realized that the hotel security staff was already stampeding in his direction. Heather watched as he dashed from the darkness around the porch steps and ran, crouching, for the small private-parking area behind the building.

Jake leaped to his feet, aiming not at the poor target of the running man but at the steady unmoving target presented by the jeep. Carefully he stood, feet braced, and fired once, twice, three times into the front wheels of the vehicle.

Monroe leaped for the seat, slamming the ignition. The engine squealed protestingly to life but the jeep raced forward for only a few yards before another of Jake's shots caught it. This time one of the tires seemed to explode. There was a screech as Monroe fought for control and lost. The vehicle slowed to a stop just as the three security guards converged on it.

"Watch it, he's armed!"

Jake's shouted warning slowed the uniformed men but they didn't stop. Revolvers raised, they approached with caution.

"You in the jeep. Out!" The man in charge of the three guards barked an order that was obeyed very slowly a few minutes later.

Rick Monroe tossed down his gun and stood scowling furiously in the pale gleam of the overhead parking lot light. The security guards surrounded him instantly. Heather ignored the scene, struggling to her feet and reaching for Jake.

"Jake, are you all right? I thought I felt something hit you."

Jake lowered the gun in his hand, aware of the chill that climbed his arm and radiated into his shoulder. His head began a slow steady spin that annoyed him enormously. There was something he had to do, something that had to be said.

"You've been hit!" Heather's expression went from concern to horror. "Your arm. You're bleeding!" Her hand came up to clamp over the source of the numbing cold and Jake followed the action as if it were all happening in slow motion.

"Heather, I want to tell you . . ."

"Hush, darling. Can you make it to the steps?"

He ignored that. "No, this is more important. Listen to me, dammit!" Her pale face was swimming in and out of the fog that was starting to cloud his vision, and Jake felt a sense of panic. So much to say and he couldn't wait any longer. What if he never came out of the fog? And the pain was starting. Oh, God, the pain. It became even more difficult to think.

"Lie down, Jake. One of the guards is calling an ambulance. They've gone to get some bandages."

"Heather, shut up and listen to me." But she had him down on the porch, flat on his back. Her hand was still clamped around his arm with a fierceness that fascinated him. She was so strong in so many ways. In the moonlight he could see his blood welling up between her fingers.

"I'm listening, Jake," she said gently.

"Heather, I love you."

There, it had been said. The crucial message conveyed, Jake gave up the battle against shock and pain and let himself slip into the soothing darkness of unconsciousness.

HEATHER WAS SITTING by his bedside the next time Jake opened his eyes. She felt his hand tighten convulsively around hers and then his lashes lifted uncertainly.

"About time you woke up," she murmured as he slowly focused on her.

Jake stared at her as though he wasn't quite sure she was real. Then he scanned his surroundings.

"Hospital?" he got out a little hoarsely.

"I'm afraid so. Cheer up, though, you had the good taste to collapse away from the guests." She looked at him with love, concealing the tremendous relief she felt now that he was conscious again. The doctor had assured her Jake would be fine but until he had opened his eyes, she could not relax.

"Mustn't disturb the guests," he agreed slowly. "What time is it?" He searched her face as if he expected to be able to tell the hour from looking at her.

"Six o'clock. It's morning, Jake. Last night was when it all happened. You haven't lost more than a few hours." She sensed his feeling of disorientation.

He frowned intently. "Last night. You came to me last night."

"Yes." Her mouth curved gently.

"And tore up the contract. You're going to marry me."

"Mother's going to spend the day rescheduling the wedding for the end of next week," she assured him.

"You'll be there this time, won't you?"

"Yes."

"Because you love me," he concluded.

"Oh, yes, Jake. I love you."

"I knew for sure last night." He closed his eyes again and Heather worried that he might go back to sleep. But a moment later he opened them. "I should have been certain that first time. You're too strong, too proud to surrender for any other reason."

"So are you," she said quietly.

"I wanted to, Heather. God knows I wanted to. I just didn't know how. Until you showed me last night. Did I tell you I love you?"

"Just before you passed out."

"Good. I knew I'd said the words but I wasn't sure if you heard them. I meant them, Heather."

"I know. If I'd been thinking straight I would have realized that what you felt for me was love. I wouldn't have needed to hear the words. But I was running blind myself until the very last."

The half smile quirked his lips. "A heck of a team."

Heather lifted one shoulder in arrogant dismissal. "So there were a few minor details that we had to work out. I think things will function very well from now on."

"Just keep telling me you love me," he insisted.

"Forever," she vowed.

"And I'll keep saying the same thing to you," he promised earnestly. He was silent for a moment, his lashes falling softly against the hard plane of his cheek. "I love you so much, honey."

"Jake, does your arm hurt very badly?" Heather frowned in concern at the tightly drawn lines around his mouth.

"Not as long as you're holding my other hand. They got Monroe okay?"

"You got Monroe. The guards just rounded him up after you'd stopped him. Since when did you start carrying a gun, Jake Cavender?"

"Since we got back from the canyon. I had security on full alert. Don't know how that jeep got through." Jake moved his head in obvious annoyance.

"Watson, the head of security, says Monroe didn't come through the main entrance. He came the back way, across Winthrop land."

"There's no road."

"He didn't need one with the four-wheel drive."

"Wait until I get my hands on Watson and his crew. I gave them specific instructions to keep a close eye on your cottage until we'd heard Monroe and his friend had been picked up."

"You suspected Rick might come back for me?"

Jake muttered something explicit. "It was a possibility. You were really the only witness he had to worry about. You knew him and he'd talked enough to give you an idea of what he and his pal were doing."

"Why on earth didn't you tell me you were taking all those precautions?" Heather scolded.

"Didn't want you to worry. I just wanted you to concentrate on making a decision about us. I was too busy trying to corner you to bother warning you," he ended roughly.

"The warning wouldn't have done any good. I'd still have been knocking on your door last night and we'd still have made love and you'd still have walked me back to my cottage." Heather shuddered. "I didn't even see Rick until he ran for the jeep. That bullet you took was meant for me."

"Any word on his pal?" He ignored her last comment.

"One of the cops who came to the hospital earlier said they picked up a Joseph Kincaid trying to cross the border last night. He's wanted on several counts of drug dealing, I gather. They think he's the 'Joe' who was associated with Rick."

"What are you thinking, Heather?" Jake demanded as she fell thoughtfully silent.

"I was wondering why Rick bothered to come back. He told me up at the cabin that he was going to be retiring in Mexico on what he'd earned on drugs. Why did he take the risk of coming after me?"

"Because he either decided he wanted the freedom to go back and forth across the border in case he changed his mind or because—" Jake stopped.

"Because what?"

"Maybe he wanted revenge for the fact that you escaped him twice. The first time you were supposed to be his meal ticket and the second time you were a witness who could do some real damage. Who knows? So Ruth is replanning the wedding, hmm?" He looked content for a moment.

"She certainly is. She's going to have Julian prepare the entire reception menu again. I still feel terrible about what must have happened to all the goodies he fixed the first time!"

"Don't worry, he'll be delighted," Jake said dryly. "And doubly so since he found out you've approved all his new menus."

Heather smiled. "I think it's time you got some more sleep. You look a little peaked, to put it mildly."

"I shouldn't be feeling this drowsy," he complained. "What have they got me on, anyway?"

"Something to keep you off your feet for a while. Don't worry about it, Jake. Just go back to sleep."

"And where are you going?"

"Nowhere."

His hand tightened on hers in thanks. "I love you, Heather."

"You're getting very good at saying that."

"And I'll get even better. It gets easier with repetition. I'll be practicing a lot."

He was asleep when the young nurse came into the room fifteen minutes later. "How's our patient?" she asked cheerfully.

"He woke up for a few minutes."

"I assume he sounded reasonably rational?" The nurse checked the bandages on Jake's arm.

"Never more so."

"Good. Maybe you should go catch a nap yourself, Miss Strand. You've been awake all night and it's almost time for breakfast."

"I told him I'd stay here." Heather didn't move.

The young woman grinned. "Like that, is it?"

Heather nodded. "We're partners, you see. A team."

THE WEDDING WENT OFF with picture-perfect precision. The bride arrived at the chapel on her father's arm in plenty of time to walk demurely down the aisle.

There she was sedately handed over to a groom who was clearly not expecting any last-minute complications this time around. The sisters of the bride smiled with delight. The mother of the bride cried and the father watched fondly as his daughter was joined in matrimony to the man he had handpicked for her.

Afterward nearly two hundred people swamped the terrace on which the reception was being held. Julian Richards beamed as his exquisitely prepared food was consumed in massive quantities.

The entire scene was everything a family could wish for its beloved daughter. True, the groom still had his arm in a sling, but that didn't prevent him from maintaining a lovingly possessive eye on his charming bride. In fact, he didn't allow her more than a foot from his side the entire time.

It was nearly two o'clock when Heather finally slipped away with the aid of her sisters and changed into a lightweight yellow pantsuit with a rakishly wide leather belt. Jake was waiting for her as she kissed her mother goodbye. Then he led her through the hail of rice to the Mercedes.

Safely ensconced on the seat beside him, Heather grinned unabashedly at her new husband. "How did I do?"

"Let's see," he said thoughtfully as he guided the car out of the parking lot. "No showing up at the wedding on a black motorcycle, no major scenes, no high drama, no wrestling with the groom in front of the guests. Not too bad, actually. A little dull from the point of view of some of the guests, perhaps, but everything was perfect as far as I was concerned."

Heather laughed delightedly. "Do you really think some of the guests were disappointed?"

"Well, they have come to expect fireworks and excitement from Heather Strand."

"Now that she's Heather Strand Cavender, they'll see a new me."

"Don't go promising anything rash. I rather like the old Heather."

"Probably just as well. I'm afraid she's still very much a part of me. I heard Cecil Winthrop asking how you intended to perform your husbandly duties with that sling on your arm."

"Cecil was a bit tipsy, I'm afraid."

"I know. But you answered him. I saw you. What did you tell him, Jake?"

Jake tossed her a charmingly arrogant, thoroughly masculine grin that somehow managed to convey all the vast love he held for his new wife.

"I told him love would find a way."

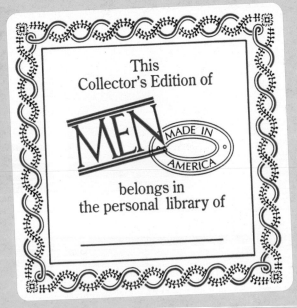

This
Collector's Edition of

MEN
MADE IN
AMERICA

belongs in
the personal library of

_____